ELYSiUM

CATHERINE JINKS was born in Brisbane in 1963 and grew up in Sydney and Papua New Guinea. She studied medieval history at university, and her love of reading led her to become a writer. She lives in the Blue Mountains in New South Wales with her Canadian husband, Peter, and her daughter, Hannah.

Catherine Jinks is the author of over twenty books for children and adults, including the award-winning Pagan series.

ELYSIUM

CASE
#4

Allie's Ghost Hunters

CATHERINE JINKS

ALLEN&UNWIN

To Joshua Burrows, who sent me a fan letter without a return address.
Sorry it took so long to get back to you.

First published in 2007

Copyright © Catherine Jinks, 2007

Allen & Unwin
83 Alexander St
Crows Nest NSW 2065
Australia
Phone: (61 2) 8425 0100
Fax: (61 2) 9906 2218
Email: info@allenandunwin.com
Web: www.allenandunwin.com

National Library of Australia
Cataloguing-in-Publication entry:
Jinks, Catherine, 1963– .
Elysium : a ghost story.

For children.
ISBN 9781741140811.

1. Ghosts – Juvenile fiction. 2. Jenolan Caves (N.S.W.) – Juvenile fiction. I. Title.
(Series : Jinks, Catherine, 1963- Allie's ghost hunters).

A823.3

Cover design by Tabitha King
Text design by Jo Hunt and Tabitha King
Set in 13 on 15.5pt Weiss by Midland Typesetters, Australia
Printed in Australia by McPherson's Printing Group

10 9 8 7 6 5 4 3 2 1

ELYSIUM, *n. - 1.* The abode assigned to the blessed after death in Greek mythology. Also *transf.* of other states of the departed. *2. fig.* A place or state of ideal happiness.

Minutes of the Ninth General Meeting of the Exorcists' Club, held at Alethea Gebhardt's house

1. The President (Alethea Gebhardt) declared the meeting open.

2. The Secretary (Bettina Berich) read out her minutes from the last meeting.

3. The Publicity Officer (Michelle du Moulin) wanted to know if the Club's members had asked their parents about the Jenolan Caves Ghost Tour, as mentioned at the last meeting.

4. The Treasurer (Peter Cresciani) replied that his parents couldn't afford a trip like that.

5. Bettina said that her mum couldn't afford it either.

6. Alethea said that her mum was really keen to go, but not because of the Ghost Tour. According to Alethea's mum, the Jenolan Caves are a natural wonder that everyone should see, ghosts or no ghosts.

7. Michelle said that she and her mum were definitely going. She pointed out that because the trip was being organised as a group tour by Paranormal Research Investigation Services and Monitoring (PRISM), the rooms had been booked at a slightly cheaper rate.

8. Bettina said that she still couldn't go.

9. Peter said that, even at a cheaper rate, the trip would be much too expensive for a family of seven — like his own. He complained that it wasn't fair. He really, really wanted to go, because the Jenolan Caves Ghost Tour sounded super-spooky.

10. Alethea promised to write a detailed report about the trip for Peter and Bettina, since any information on the subject of ghosts would be important to them as members of the Exorcists' Club.

11. It was agreed that this report would be read out at the very next meeting.

12. No one had any other business to discuss, so the meeting was adjourned, and everyone went down to the kitchen to eat banana muffins.

The President's Report to the Exorcists' Club
by Alethea Gebhardt

CHAPTER # one

We left home on Saturday morning, in Ray's car. Mum's car is an old bomb; it's been having 'tummy troubles', according to Mum. She was afraid that its insides would suddenly fall out onto the road, halfway up a mountain. That's why we took Ray's car. It belongs to the Department of Forestry, so it's in pretty good shape. If it wasn't, he wouldn't be able to draw so many trees.

(That's his job, in case I never told you. Drawing trees in national parks. That's what he does when he isn't painting pictures.)

The trip took about four hours. It would have been shorter if we hadn't stopped for lunch. Bethan also had to keep going to the toilet – or so he said.

Personally, I think he just wanted to get out of the car. He's a very restless traveller, for someone who's nearly nine years old. He can't just sit back and listen to a CD. Oh, no. He's always wanting muesli bars, or lemonade, or a game of 'I Spy'. Then, when he gets *really* bored, he starts poking me with his foot. Just to start an argument.

He finds arguments much more entertaining than scenery. Most boys of his age are like that, I've noticed. They won't spend more than five seconds looking at a view, but they have to wrestle with someone at least three times a day. If only I had two brothers instead of one, they could wrestle with each other, and then I wouldn't have to put up with so much poking and prodding.

We ate lunch in the Blue Mountains. Mum had packed us a picnic, with wholemeal bread and apples, but at least she bought us some ice-cream as well. I had a chocolate ice-cream, and Bethan's was blue. He smeared it all over his T-shirt, and dripped it onto Mum's white shorts. That's when she told him that she wouldn't be getting any more blue ice-cream. It was unhealthy, she said – full of additives. I guess she must have been right, because the next day Bethan came running out of the toilet, exclaiming that his poo was bright green.

But I'm getting ahead of myself.

We reached the Jenolan Caves just after two

o'clock in the afternoon. To get to the caves, you have to drive over a series of rolling hills, before plunging down, down, down into a very long, deep valley, with a small river running through it. The lower you go, the shadier it gets. The road is really narrow, with a lot of hair-pin bends, and Ray was sweating by the time we hit the bottom. But what we saw then was well worth the strain on his nerves, because we found ourselves face-to-face with an enormous tunnel. You've never seen anything like this tunnel. It's the height of a six-storeyed building, and carved into a sheer wall of rock. You can drive your car right through it. In fact we *did* drive our car right through it.

'This is the Grand Arch,' said Ray, as we crawled along in the dimness. 'I remember this.'

'Is it one of the caves?' asked Bethan.

'The caves are mostly underground,' Mum replied, and suddenly we were in the sunshine again, surrounded by people and buildings and footpaths and signs. Ahead of us was something that looked like a gigantic half-timbered mansion, with red umbrellas lined up in front of it. This, according to Ray, was the famous Jenolan Caves House. He turned left before he reached it, and parked in the guests' car park, which was chiselled into a hillside behind the hotel.

The minute I got out of the car, I knew that we

3

were somewhere special. There was a feeling about the place. The valley walls were so high and close that they seemed to be nudging at your heels. It was like being in a pocket. We passed a mysterious door in a cliff-face as we made our way out of the car park. High above, a scattering of little houses clung desperately to the bushy slopes. Trees were pressing in on all sides. Rounding a corner, we found ourselves back on the road. To our right, the Grand Arch loomed mysteriously.

'Look! Look!' cried Bethan. 'There's that arch again!'

'We'll look at it later,' said Ray. 'Right now we have to get our room sorted out.'

'Are the underground caves as big as that arch? Mum? Are they all like that?'

'I can't remember, Bethan. I don't think so. We'll find out soon, okay? After we unpack.'

So we went into Caves House. It's the only place you can stay at, around there. Its reception hall has fake marble pillars, and a parquet floor, and a sweeping staircase. There's also a gift shop opening off the hall.

Bethan headed straight for the gift shop, naturally.

'Bethan!' Mum yelled, when she realised where he was. 'Allie, will you go and get him, please? We'll check out the gift shop later.'

4

'Okay.'

'Tell him we have to get organised, and *then* we can have – oh! Hi, Richard!'

Richard Boyer had suddenly emerged from the gift shop. For those of you who haven't met Richard (like Bettina, for instance), let me just say that he's very tall and thin, with bright blue eyes, curly hair, and glasses. I guess he was hanging around the reception hall because he had organised the tour, and felt that he ought to be on hand when everyone arrived. Richard is a long-time member of PRISM; he takes it very seriously.

The woman with him was quite short. She had wavy brown hair caught up in a barrette, and a calm face, and dark eyes. She also wore glasses. I don't know if it was the glasses, or the way she was leaning against him, but as soon as I saw her I knew that she must be Richard's new girlfriend. Mum had mentioned something about Richard bringing his new girlfriend.

That's probably why his old girlfriend hadn't wanted to come. Even though she's psychic, and knows a lot about ghosts.

'Judy!' said Richard. 'Ray! You got here!'

'Are we the first?' Mum asked.

'No, no. We're only waiting on a couple more people. Jim Bainbridge and . . . Matsumoto something?'

'Matoaka,' I corrected. 'Her name's Matoaka.'

Mum rolled her eyes. Matoaka is my dad's girl-friend. He brought her over here from Thailand a few months ago, but she's not Asian or anything. She's from Brisbane, and her real name's Maureen.

Dad's not from Thailand either, by the way. He went there when I was four. Ever since he came back, there have been problems. (Peter knows about some of them.) Dad and Mum have been arguing a lot, lately, because after so many years away from us, Dad now wants to have a say in our lives. Mum keeps telling him that this is 'unacceptable'. Whereupon Dad replies that he's never missed a single child support payment, and therefore still has some rights as a father.

I don't know what to think, really. Except that I'm glad we don't have to live with him. It annoyed me when I heard that he was doing the Jenolan Caves Ghost Tour. I knew there would be arguments if he turned up.

As far as I can see, he only decided to come because he wanted to show us how involved he was in our lives.

'Oh,' said Richard. 'So you know these people, do you?'

'I should,' Mum replied. 'Jim's my ex. Didn't he tell you?'

'No, he just – no.' Richard flushed, pushing his

6

glasses up his nose. He's very pale, and he flushes a lot. 'Uh – this is Rosemary, by the way,' he continued, as he flung his arm around his new girlfriend. 'I've told her all about you guys. She's been dying to meet you.'

'Hi,' said Rosemary, shyly.

'Hi,' said Mum. (Ray was talking to the girl behind the reception desk.)

'Rosemary works for the Heritage and Conservation branch of the Department of Environment and Planning,' Richard went on. 'So of course she wanted to see the Jenolan Caves. It's a very important historical site.'

'Not to mention stunning,' said Mum. 'I'd forgotten how beautiful it is. So atmospheric.'

Everyone nodded. Taking advantage of this brief pause, I asked, 'Has Michelle arrived yet?'

Richard just blinked at me.

'Michelle du Moulin?' I pressed. 'You've met her? She's my friend.'

'Oh! The du Moulins!' he exclaimed. 'Party of three! Yes, they're here – somewhere. I've told everyone to meet in the dining room at six, so you'll see 'em there, I should think.'

Party of three? And then I remembered – Sylvester. Of course.

Michelle had been complaining about Sylvester. He was her mum's new boyfriend. Michelle was furious that he had decided to 'mess up the weekend' by coming along too.

'Right!' said Ray, turning his back on the reception desk. He was jangling a set of keys. 'All sorted. Let's go. Hi, Richard.'

'Hi, Ray. This is Rosemary.'

'Hi, Rosemary.'

'Allie,' said Mum, 'will you *please* fetch Bethan? I already asked you once.'

It was hard to drag Bethan away from the gift shop. When I finally got him into the reception hall, he spotted a display of crystals and stalactites in a glass case, and I had to push him past that, too. But we reached the stairs eventually. Then he raced us all to the first floor, where he disappeared into a room on the right. It contained a billiard table.

'Mum! Mum! Look!'

'Come here, Bethan.'

'We can play snooker!'

'Not now, we can't,' said Mum.

'Our room's on the top floor, Bethan,' said Ray. 'We'll look at this later.'

'Don't worry, Mum,' I said loudly. 'If he's slow, I'll get first choice with the beds.'

That did the trick. Bethan shot out of the billiard room and surged up the next flight of stairs like a greyhound. When at last we caught up with him, he was bouncing off the green-and-white walls of a long, narrow corridor.

'Which room? Which one?' he yelped. (He was *really* over-excited.)

'As long as it's not room 104,' said Mum.

'Why?' I asked. 'What's wrong with that room?'

'It's supposed to be haunted.'

'*Really?*'

'So Richard says. He wanted Room 123, though he didn't get it. *That's* supposed to be haunted, too. They call it Miss Chisolm's room.' Mum wrapped her arms around herself, as if she were cold. 'Personally, I'd rather have a good night's sleep.'

'*I* wouldn't!' cried Bethan. 'I want to see the ghost!'

'Well you can't,' said Ray. 'Because they didn't give us room 104.' And he unlocked the door to the room they *did* give us, which didn't look particularly spooky to me. It had pale green curtains, and a green dado around the wall. The carpet was reddish, but not blood-coloured. There were two double beds and one single; Bethan wriggled past Ray and threw himself onto the closest double bed.

'Bags this bed!' he cried.

Mum and I exchanged glances.

'It's all right,' I sighed. 'He can have it.' As a mature twelve-year-old, I no longer felt the need to

9

argue about double beds. 'Where's the bathroom?'

'We share one,' Mum informed me. 'It's just down the hall.'

'Where's the television?' Bethan demanded.

'There isn't one.' Ray heaved our suitcase onto the bed nearest the window. 'You won't need one. There'll be too much else to do.'

Bethan's jaw dropped. I decided to visit the bathroom, before he began to protest. On the way, however, I was distracted by the pictures that hung in the corridor. They were photos of Caves House, going back to the nineteenth century. There was one of Caves House in 1885 (single storey, shingle roof); and another of the two-storeyed timber hotel (destroyed by fire in the 1890s); and a shot of the limestone structure built in 1907; and Caves House with its 1912 extension.

I studied these photographs with interest. Clearly, Caves House had a lot of history. But was it really haunted?

I would have to ask about this 'Miss Chisolm' person.

'Hi,' said a voice.

I jumped, and turned. Michelle was coming out of the bathroom. Her hair was wet, and she was carrying a towel.

'Michelle! Hi!'

'Did you just get here?'

'Yes. Just now. What about you?'

'Oh, *hours* ago.'

'It's great, isn't it?'

'Do you think so?' She made a face. '*I* don't. Do you realise we have to *share a bathroom?*'

You might not be aware that Michelle's mum has her own ensuite off her bedroom, at home. Since Michelle is an only child, this means that she never has to share a bathroom.

Except when she comes to our house.

'Oh, it can't be so bad,' I said.

'Have you seen it?'

'No, but –'

'Take a look. It's *disgusting.*'

Actually, the bathroom wasn't *that* terrible. Just old-fashioned. The tiles were pink and blue, the cubicles were divided by slabs of pebblecrete, and there was a laundry basket in one corner.

'It could be worse,' I pointed out. 'At least it's only for girls. Imagine if we had to share with the boys, as well.'

'It's unsanitary,' Michelle complained. 'I'll probably catch tinea.'

I looked at her hard, then, and realised that she was actually cross about something else.

'Did Sylvester come?' I asked cautiously. Sure enough, Michelle began to scowl.

'What do *you* think?' she snapped.

'Where is he now?'

'I don't know and I don't care.' Suddenly her scowl dissolved into a malicious grin. 'He was really cross,' she gloated, 'because there's no spa bath. He was expecting a spa bath.'

'Oh,' I said.

'Come and see my room. It's just down the hall.'

When Michelle said 'my room', I thought she meant the room that she was sharing with her mum and her mum's boyfriend. I wasn't expecting to enter a room containing one double bed.

'Is there a fold-out, or something?' I asked.

'What do you mean?'

'Well – where are you going to sleep?'

Michelle stared at me as if I was wearing a lobster on my head.

'I'm sleeping on the bed, of course,' she replied.

'You mean – you've got your *very own room*?'

Michelle sniffed. 'What else? Do you think they'd want me barging in on their rom-a-a-antic weekend?'

Poor Michelle. She sounded really vicious. So I tried to change the subject.

'Richard told us that this place is haunted,' I said. 'Rooms 104 and 123.'

'Did he bring his equipment?'

'I don't know.' Michelle was talking about

Richard's infra-red camera, and his electro-magnetic field detector. He uses them whenever he's hunting down ghosts for PRISM. Richard often does this kind of work in his spare time. So does Sylvia Klineberg, who was supposed to be doing the Ghost Tour as well. 'Have you seen Sylvia, yet?'

'Who?'

'You know. Sylvia. I told you about her. She came to our house once, when we were trying to get Eglantine's ghost out of Bethan's bedroom . . .'

But Michelle wasn't listening. Her mother was addressing her from the room next door.

'Michelle? Is that you, my sweet?'

Michelle didn't reply. Instead, she dragged me over to her bed. I thought: oh, no. Because she had a very mulish expression on her face.

'Come and see this little torch I bought,' she said to me. 'It's really cool.'

'Michelle? My darling?'

'Michelle, I think your mum wants you.'

'Really?' said Michelle, picking the torch off her bedside table. It looked exactly like a lipstick case on a keyring. 'I guess I couldn't hear her. Since I'm in a different *room*, and all.'

'Michelle!' Michelle's mum suddenly stuck her head around the door. She looked a little more done-up than usual. I mean, she's always beautifully

13

groomed and everything, but she doesn't normally wear such glossy lipstick or such big earrings or so many gold bracelets on her wrists. Not when she picks Michelle up from our house, anyway. 'Oh, hello, Allie,' she said. 'How are you?'

'Good.'

'Settling in all right?'

'I guess.'

'It's not quite what we expected, is it, Michelle?'

'What – you mean because there's no spa bath?' Michelle smirked. Her mother's lips tightened.

'The bathroom situation – yes,' she said, in even tones. 'I was going to ask, Michelle, if you wanted to borrow my hair dryer?'

'No, thanks.'

'Your hair's wet.'

'It'll dry.'

'Well – okay.' Michelle's mum threw up her hands. 'I tried.'

My heart sank as she withdrew. I could see that Michelle wasn't going to be having much fun at the Jenolan Caves – she was too upset about Sylvester.

And then, to make matters worse, my dad arrived.

I heard his voice while Michelle was demonstrating her new keyring torch (which had three different light filters, for pink, blue and yellow beams). When I peered out of Michelle's room, I saw that the adults were all gathered in the corridor. Mum was reluctantly introducing Dad to Michelle's mum. Michelle's mum was eagerly introducing Sylvester to my mum. Dad was introducing Matoaka to just about everybody.

Sylvester was a tall, skinny man with a big nose and a black goatee. He looked very tanned – especially standing next to my mother. (Redheads aren't supposed to go out in the sun a lot. If they do, they get skin cancer.) As for Matoaka, you wouldn't believe what she was wearing. I mean, my mum's a bit of a hippy, at heart, but I've never seen her with feathers tied to her hair. *Or* hanging off the bottom of her skirt. Matoaka was also dressed in tie-dyed stockings, beaded moccasins, and a really pretty Thai silk blouse.

She was talking about the 'totemic vibrations' of the Jenolan Caves – which she'd never visited before.

'They're so powerful,' she exclaimed. 'You can *feel* the spirit of the Dreaming, can't you? I mean, I find it hard to *breathe*, I really do. The air is so thick with energy.'

'I guess that's why it's such a good place for ghosts,' Ray remarked politely, and Dad snorted.

'This whole ghost thing is so insulting,' he said. 'Most of the time it's just a western construct imposed upon a traditional, mythic heritage. This land is of great significance, but not because of any *ghosts*. Its transcendental quality is derived from its place in Aboriginal spirituality. All this business of ghost tours and haunted hotels – it's so trashy and commercial.'

'Then why don't you just turn around and go back home?' my mother asked, in a dangerous sort of voice.

'Because I have every right to be here,' Dad replied. 'I want to know what sort of things my children are getting involved in.'

'Oh really?' Mum folded her arms. 'Is that why you vanished from their lives for eight years?'

'Guys . . . please,' said Ray. 'This isn't useful. Not now . . .'

I groaned to myself, before hiding in Michelle's bedroom. To have Michelle fighting with her mum was bad enough. To have Dad fighting with *my* mum was even worse. It wasn't going to improve our weekend, that was for sure.

Talk about atmosphere. I didn't see how Richard was going to pick up any paranormal signals, when the air was already humming with tension and bad feelings.

Besides, I thought, what ghost would put up with all the noise?

CHAPTER # two

You can guess what happened next. After everyone had found their rooms, and unpacked, and
changed, it was about half past three. Two and a
half hours to go until dinner, in other words. So
what were we all going to do?

Mum thought a bushwalk would be nice. Bethan
wanted to look at the tunnel. I was more interested
in exploring the hotel. (I still had to find out about
Miss Chisolm, and Room 123.) We were discussing our options when Dad knocked on the door,
and asked us what our plans were. He and Matoaka
wanted to join us.

'It's such a beautiful day,' he said serenely, 'that
I think it would be a good idea to get out into the

17

fresh air, after such a long drive. Don't you, Judy?'

Now, it just so happens that Mum had said *exactly* the same thing to me, about two minutes beforehand. But she obviously didn't want to admit it. In fact she didn't want Dad along at all – I could tell from her expression.

Come to think of it, she hasn't had much to do with Dad since he came back to Australia. Normally she only sees him when Bethan and I are being picked up, or dropped off. This would be the first time they had spent any amount of time together for at least eight years.

'Actually, Bethan wants to look at the tunnel,' she replied stiffly. 'I don't know if that'll be airy enough for you.'

'The tunnel?' said Dad, and Bethan hurried to explain.

'You know,' he said. 'The big one you drive through.'

'Oh.' Dad nodded. 'You mean the Devil's Coach-house.'

'Is that what it's called?' said Bethan, his eyes glinting. 'Wow!'

'Uh – actually, that one's the Grand Arch,' Ray mumbled, from one corner of the room. 'The Devil's Coach-house is something different. But we can go there too,' he added hastily. 'It's very *close* to the Grand Arch.'

Dad looked cross. Mum looked pleased. Suddenly, I wanted to get out. I really, *really* can't stand that kind of bickering and sniping. Bethan is lucky, because he usually doesn't notice. But I decided that, if Dad insisted on joining our party, then I would have to hide out with Michelle.

'If you don't mind, I'd better just see what Michelle's doing,' I said.

'Well, I don't know, Alethea.' Dad pulled a long face. 'We've come all this way for a chance to explore the natural world together, haven't we? I mean, you can always see your friends at school –'

'Oh, don't be ridiculous, Jim, of course she can go,' my mother interrupted. Breezily, she waved her hand. 'Off you trot, Allie. Just remember – be back at the dining room by six.'

I scurried away, before Dad could start arguing about the amount of time I spent with Mum compared to the amount of time I spent with him. (I'm so sick of the whole subject!) But when I found Michelle sulking in her bedroom over a Jenolan Caves brochure, she gave me the bad news. Her mum had decided to have a massage, and Sylvester was complaining of a headache. So Michelle had been given a choice: either she could stay in her room reading brochures, or come along with my family.

She came along with my family.

In the end, it wasn't too bad. The Grand Arch was only a short walk away, so there wasn't enough time to start an argument before we were suddenly swallowed up by this enormous, shadowy cavern. Then we had to concentrate on not getting hit by the cars that were winding their way through the Arch – because the cars and pedestrians all had to share one narrow road. Finally, when we reached the sheltered spot where many of the tour groups started, we were too busy talking about the Arch itself to worry about who was being unfair to whom.

'Look,' said Mum, her voice echoing slightly. She was pointing at a cluster of people who were walking down a flight of stairs high overhead. 'They must have just finished a tour.'

'Are there more caves?' asked Bethan. 'Through that door?'

'There are at least 250 caves,' Michelle replied – and, when everyone stared at her in amazement, she added, 'I read it in a brochure.'

'Only some of them are open to the public,' said Ray. 'Apparently, people are discovering new caves all the time.'

'I wish *I* could discover a new cave,' said Bethan, wistfully.

We spent about six or seven minutes slowly walking through the Grand Arch, before emerging into the sunshine again. On the other side of the Arch we found a long stretch of river between drooping ferns. The river was very, very blue – almost as blue as Bethan's ice-cream had been. Dad explained that the blue colour came from a high concentration of calcium carbonate. Above us, people were spilling out of doors in the cliff face, clattering down metal staircases and plunging back into the rock again. A few people also seemed to be disappearing down a path that wandered off to our left.

So we followed them.

First we climbed a few stairs. Next we passed a little stone utilities house, with a metal roll-a-door. Finally, we turned a bushy corner – and gasped as another great rent in the hillside opened up before us. The path headed straight into it.

'Oh, wow,' said Bethan.

'What's that?' said Michelle.

'That's the Devil's Coach-house,' said Dad, reading from a sign that stood beside our path.

The Devil's Coach-house started off quite narrow and dark, but widened into a huge light-filled chamber with a small hole in its ceiling. It was like walking through a big throat into an enormous open mouth. The mouth was dribbling dusty grey stalactites – so many stalactites that its roof appeared to be melting. There were big holes poked into its walls, as if by a giant finger. The floor was covered in a tumble of loose boulders, most of them highly polished. Rusting metal spikes stuck out of some, while others bore a blush of yellow lichen.

We all stood speechless, until Bethan caught sight of Richard Boyer.

'Look!' he cried, and laughed at the echo produced by his voice. 'Hey!' (*Ey*, sighed the cave.) 'There's Richard!' (*Ichard . . .*)

Richard was with Rosemary. They were holding hands, and I don't know if they really wanted to have us barging in on them. But they were very polite. In fact Richard told us how the Devil's Coach-house had been named.

'It was because of a bloke called Luke White,' he said. 'He was a cattle thief, and one night he slept here after a drinking binge. In the middle of the night he woke up and saw six horses drawing a coach around the cave. The horses were being driven by the Devil. When he told people about it, the name stuck.'

'*Cool*,' said Bethan. But Mum wasn't impressed.

'After a drinking binge, did you say?' she drawled. 'Sounds like the alcohol talking, to me.'

Richard smiled.

'I certainly don't think PRISM would regard Luke White as a reliable eyewitness,' he conceded.

'What about the Aboriginal name?' Matoaka asked, earnestly. 'Do you know what that is?'

'Uh – no.' Richard turned to his girlfriend. 'Do you?'

'The caves were called Binoomea,' she said. 'I'm not sure about the Devil's Coach-house. Though I do know the whole place was supposed to have been formed by Gurangatch. He was a sort of Rainbow Serpent. Half fish, half reptile.'

'Rosemary was once involved in listing an Aboriginal sacred site, up near Katoomba,' Richard explained proudly, and Matoaka caught her breath.

'Oh,' she gasped. 'What an *honour!*'

'Yes.' Rosemary smiled her shy smile. 'It was.'

'I'm an old soul myself,' Matoaka continued, 'so I can always see ancient energy in other people. Do you have a blood connection, or is it purely spiritual?'

Rosemary blinked. She looked confused. Richard said, 'I – I don't think Rosemary has any Aboriginal ancestors. If that's what you mean.'

'My own spirit guide is Powhatan,' said Matoaka. 'Native American. But I'm open to the harmonic force of the sacred in every culture.'

'Matoaka has very strong shamanic skills,' Dad added.

No one knew what to say to this. So after a

23

brief pause, I asked Richard the question I'd been wanting to ask for a while.

'Who's Miss Chisolm?'

His face brightened.

'Ah! Well, Miss Chisolm is the most famous ghost at Cave House. She worked there until 1965. The dining room is called Chisolm's because her ghost is supposed to be always rearranging the table in the far right-hand corner, after the room has been locked.'

'Co-*ool*,' said Bethan.

'The trouble is that most of the apparitions seen around Cave House have been in the form of a woman dressed in *nineteenth-century* clothes,' Richard went on. 'So it's been argued that the ghost is actually that of Lucinda Wilson, who was the wife of the caves' first caretaker, Jeremiah Wilson. Though the dog was probably Miss Chisolm's.'

'The dog?' said Ray.

'Every now and then, someone sees a dog in one of the car parks,' Richard explained happily. 'Because it's a national park around here, a ranger gets called in to deal with it, but the dog always disappears.' Pushing his glasses up his nose, Richard grinned at Bethan. 'Whenever the dog appears, strange things also happen in the dining room. Then someone found a photo of Miss Chisolm with her dog, and . . . well, they drew the obvious conclusion.'

Michelle and I exchanged glances. We were both impressed. Clearly, Richard had picked the perfect spot for a PRISM outing. The Jenolan Caves had to be crawling with ghosts.

'Are you making this up?' Dad asked, sceptically.

'I'm not,' Richard replied. 'I can't speak for the sources. Most of the houses around here – the ones belonging to guides past and present – are supposed to be haunted. A ghost carrying a suitcase has even been seen walking the roads. And there are the caves, of course. The caves seem to be full of ghosts, if you believe what you hear. Which I don't, necessarily.' He grinned again. 'But that's the challenge, isn't it? As a paranormal investigator, you have to sift the truth from the lies.'

I was going to ask if he had brought his equipment. Matoaka, however, jumped in first.

'If there are spirits trapped here,' she insisted, 'then they must be trapped by the force of the Dreaming. I wouldn't be surprised if a lot of ley energy paths were converging in this place – don't you think, Jim? The vibrations must be fierce. All those underground chambers must amplify the imbalance.'

Dad inclined his head. Mum cast her eyes to heaven. Richard shrugged.

'I don't know about energy paths,' he admitted. 'But I've heard it said that the Jenolan Caves cast a spell on people. They keep coming back, and finally they can't leave. Not even in death.'

Silence fell. We all looked around, feeling the weight of the fretted rock that arched over us. A nasty picture flashed into my head: a picture of the huge mouth in which we stood suddenly closing. Trapping us all inside.

I thought: if you die in the caves, do you *automatically* become a ghost? Because you aren't allowed to leave, for some reason?

'Right,' said Mum, ending the pause. 'I think it's time for a coffee, don't you?'

CHAPTER # three

That night, we ate dinner in Chisolm's dining room. Our table was in the far right-hand corner, near the window. It was pretty big because it had to accommodate fifteen people.

Richard had booked it specially. Sylvia Klineberg was there, and she greeted me with a smile. No one in my family had seen her since that business with Eglantine, last year, but she hadn't changed much. Her hair was still short and grey. She still dressed neatly. The only difference was that she didn't seem so brisk and efficient – perhaps because of her thirteen-year-old son, who had come with her.

His name was Paul, and he was a real pig. I don't know what his problem was. First he kept kicking the table leg, like someone Bethan's age. Then, when Sylvia asked him to 'Please stop, darling — there's a good boy', he started poking holes in the tablecloth with his fork. He wouldn't eat his food, either. He kept mashing it into a disgusting mulch. Finally, Sylvia gave him some of *her* food: roast lamb, I think. Paul chewed away at a few mouthfuls before spitting them out, and dumping the mangled bits of gristle on his mother's plate.

Michelle and I couldn't believe our eyes.

The other two strangers who ate with us were Gordon and Joyce. They were a retired couple, and they had been members of PRISM for years. They had also been just about everywhere. In Scotland, they had visited Loch Ness. In Queensland, they had looked for the mysterious 'Min Min' lights, which travellers in the outback are sometimes supposed to see. They had been to Nepal, to Salem (Massachusetts) and to Egypt. They had even been hypnotised, and had attended a 'past lives' workshop. Their main hobby was staying in haunted houses.

'I was sleeping in an old bed-and-breakfast once, when in the middle of the night my covers were pulled right over my face,' Joyce told us. 'As if someone was trying to make the bed. I screamed, of course, and pushed them back. But when I turned on the light, no one else was in the room.'

It was nice, being surrounded by people who believed in ghosts. Most of the time I don't talk much about Eglantine. Well, you know what it's like. If you mention the ghost that used to be in your brother's bedroom, everyone thinks you're a lunatic. That night, however, I didn't have to worry. Gordon and Joyce were eager to hear about Eglantine – as well as every other ghost I've ever had to deal with. (Note to Bettina: I think they may want to visit your house some time. Just because it was haunted, once.) Sylvia was also very interested. Even Matoaka seemed to lap it all up.

Only Dad and Paul disapproved. When Dad wasn't clicking his tongue over the fact that Bethan and I were eating red meat ('Do you know what sort of hormones get injected into that stuff?'), he kept shaking his head sadly whenever anyone mentioned the word 'ghost'. 'People shouldn't search for meaning in death, instead of life,' he lamented. 'Nothing could be more unhealthy.' It seemed odd to me that someone who lived with Matoaka should disapprove of ghost-hunting – because Matoaka, after all, had been talking about her Native American spirit guide. But perhaps Dad regarded ghosts as being different from spirits. Especially if the spirits were Native American and the ghosts were Anglo-Saxon.

At least Dad took the whole subject seriously,

though. Paul just thought we were stupid. I could tell. When he let rip a huge, stinking fart, he didn't apologise. He simply glanced around the table, with a sneer on his face, and said, 'Don't look at me. The ghost did it.'

Bethan laughed, of course. He'll laugh at anything to do with farts, I'm afraid.

As for Rosemary, I don't think she had made up her mind about ghosts one way or another. I happened to sit next to her, and she turned out to be really nice. In fact I could see why Richard preferred his new girlfriend to his old girlfriend, even though I like Delora a lot. For a start, Rosemary doesn't smoke, so she doesn't cough as much. She's also about the same age as Richard. And she's smart, too. Delora isn't dumb, but Rosemary is super-smart, like Richard. The only trouble is, she's not clever about everything. She *certainly* doesn't understand ghosts.

For instance, I overheard her talking about a dream she'd been having, almost every night for weeks, and I couldn't believe what she thought. She thought that she was going to have to make an appointment with a counsellor, or a psychiatrist.

'My grandmother's been dead for over a year,' she said to Sylvia, who was sitting across the table. 'It doesn't make sense, but I think that I must have bottled up all the grief, so I could be strong for my mother. And now I must be paying the price.' She explained that, in the dream, her dead grand- mother had been appearing at the foot of her bed, wringing her hands and crying. 'It's so real,' she finished, 'that I actually stopped sleeping in my own room. It was disturbing me too much. That's why I think I should talk to someone about it.'

Sylvia started nodding sympathetically, but I shook my head.

'You don't have to do that,' I objected. 'It's got nothing to do with *you*, I bet. It's your grand- mother. She has the problem, not you.'

Rosemary stared at me in astonishment. Sylvia winced.

'Uh – Allie . . .' she began, and I knew what she was going to say. She was going to say something about exploring all the other possibilities first. It's what she always says. But she hasn't encountered as many ghosts as I have.

'It's probably your grandmother's ghost,' I pointed out to Rosemary. 'And ghosts never turn up unless they want something. You should find out what she wants, and then she'll go away.'

Rosemary gave a kind of embarrassed half- smile. Even so, she was interested. She's one of those people who are interested in just about everything.

'Really?' she said. 'Is that what you think?'

'Oh, yes.' The fact that the dream seemed real meant that it probably *was* real, I decided. 'You're lucky, because a lot of ghosts don't actually appear like that – as a person. If you were feeling miserable all the time, or if a stain kept appearing on your blankets, that might be a ghost too. Only you wouldn't know who they were, so it would be much, much harder to find out what they wanted. Why don't you ask your grandmother what she wants, next time?'

Rosemary's mouth dropped open. Before she could reply, however, Richard stood up to make a speech. He said that he was pleased to welcome everyone to this, the second ghost tour organised for PRISM members and friends. It was gratifying to see how many people had shown up.

'Every Saturday night a ghost tour is conducted here,' Richard said. 'It's done for one simple reason: this place is notorious. There are no end of stories told about phantom tour groups, strange noises, lights going on and off – you name it. In fact they leave the lights on in the Caves House corridors at night for this very reason. Furthermore, the room in which you are actually sitting is supposed to be haunted.'

I looked around at the carved wooden mantle-piece, and the coffered ceiling, and the red-and-gold wallpaper, as Richard repeated what he'd said earlier, about the souls of people who can't bear to be parted from the Jenolan Caves. I couldn't see any pictures of Miss Chisolm anywhere. Opera music was spilling out of black speakers mounted on the walls. Around us, the other tables were filling up. Waiters hurried about laden with plates of lamb and duck and barbecued octopus.

It didn't much look like a haunted room. But at night, perhaps, when the lights were off . . .?

'Now, before I finish, I just want to run through what's going to happen after dinner,' Richard concluded. He looked slightly uncomfortable in his linen jacket, which must have been brand new; he kept scratching his neck, adjusting his cuffs and yanking at his lapels. 'At eight-thirty, we have to be waiting at the entrance to the hotel car park, under the shelter shed. That's where our guide is going to meet us. I'll be taking my electromagnetic field detector, but I doubt we'll be seeing any action. From what I can gather, most of the sightings happen when guides are alone, collecting rubbish or otherwise tidying up. Still – you never know.' He glanced around the table with a bashful grin. 'Maybe tonight we'll get lucky.'

'Here, here,' boomed Gordon, as Richard sat down. Then Sylvia tapped on her wineglass with a fork, and gave a quick speech about how grateful we were to Richard for organising this terrific opportunity. (While she was talking, Paul peeled a scab off his elbow, looking thoroughly fed up.) After that, we all ate dessert – even Michelle's mum, who's usually on a diet – before everyone rushed off to make last-minute 'preparations'.

'There are no toilets inside the caves,' Mum warned Bethan, when he protested that he didn't need to empty his bladder. Mum also went to the toilet, and made Ray change his shoes. Bethan and I had to clean our teeth, as well. There was so much to do that we were the last people to reach the car park entrance, at eight-thirty.

Even Dad was waiting there when we arrived. He was wearing the baggiest cargo pants I've ever seen.

The guide was there, too. His name was Greg. He reminded me of a teacher I once had: thin and young, with a big, white smile and lots of energy. He explained that he would be taking us through little bits of the Orient, Ribbon, River and Lucas caves as part of our ghost tour. These caves were on the southern side of the Grand Arch. According to Greg, Gurangatch, who created the caves while fleeing from the giant quoll Mirrigan, was supposed to have been a water dragon. 'And one day,' he added, 'that dragon's going to wake up and kill us all – or so the story goes.'

Paul snorted loudly. He was chewing bubblegum,

and blowing noisy bubbles. Greg asked him to please remove the gum from his mouth before entering the caves. No food or drink from this point on, said Greg, and asked if anyone had any questions.

Richard cleared his throat.

'Uh – have *you* ever experienced anything strange, underground?' he queried.

Greg smiled. 'Not me personally,' he said. 'But a lot of the other guides have. So . . .' He looked around. 'Everyone still ready to go in?'

We were. By this time the sky overhead was dark, and full of stars. It was also very quiet. Greg led us up a steep path to a door in a cliff-face, which marked the entrance to the Binoomea Cut. This tunnel had been blasted through solid rock in the 1950s, Greg informed us. (I wrote the date down in my notebook.) It was long and straight and damp, with nothing to see inside it but a series of metal doors. As we trudged along, I prayed that no one was going to be really, *really* pathetic and make a ghostly 'ooo-ing' noise.

Alas – my prayer wasn't answered. We had reached the Orient Cave when I heard it: '*Ooooo-oo.*' But to my surprise, Bethan wasn't to blame.

Paul was the culprit.

'Okay,' said Greg, ignoring this feeble attempt at humour. He had paused by a bank of electrical switches, which he began to turn on. Bursts of light flared up all around us. 'This is the Persian Chamber,' he said, 'and as you can see it's quite spectacular. The Pillar of Hercules, down there, is one of the caves' highest stalagmites. There are stories about how people who approach this chamber often hear the sound of singing – which stops as soon as they get inside. The guy who actually discovered the cave was named James Wiburd, and he was an interesting fellow. In fact, if there's anyone haunting the Jenolan Caves, it would have to be James Wiburd.'

I looked around. In the glow of the electric light, everything shone and glittered. There were formations like ice-cream cornets, like tripe, like frosting, like teeth. There were minarets and shawls. There were patches of white and pink coral.

It was amazing.

'O-o-oh,' Mum sighed. 'Oh, Ray.'

'How can anyone be interested in unnatural manifestations,' said Dad loftily, 'when the natural world is so full of wonders?'

'Look,' said Bethan. 'That bit looks just like chicken nuggets.'

Taking us through to the Egyptian and Indian chambers, Greg went on to describe how James Wiburd had been the caves' foremost explorer. But then the government destroyed a third of the

Ribbon Cave to create better access. So James had left in a rage, taking his diaries with him and covering up some of the cave entrances, vowing that no one would ever find the things he'd seen.

'Sometimes, even now, we stumble across new caves with Wiburd's name written in them,' Greg added. 'Ah. Now here's an interesting spot. This is where a guy I know kept seeing someone out of the corner of his eye. But whenever he flashed his torch towards this mysterious person, the torch went dead. The light would only come back when he shone it away from that spot.'

I looked around hastily. From where I stood, I could see ice-white stalactites, and strange, pinkish slabs of rock ribbed with narrow threads of white – like slabs of raw chicken – and weird growths all over the ground that resembled the surface of someone's brain. I could see petrified cascades of creamy calcite deposits, drooling and dripping off enormous stone wedding cakes. But I couldn't see anything ghostly. Not unless you counted the formations themselves.

Some of the stalagmites were tall and wide enough to seem vaguely human in shape. (If you were almost blind, and had very little light with you.)

Michelle made an explosive noise beside me.

'For heaven's sake,' she muttered.

Glancing back, I saw what was upsetting her. Sylvester and her mum were dawdling behind the main group, kissing and cuddling. It amazed me that they could ignore what was around them, and concentrate on each other. Neither of them looked nearly as nice as the cave did.

'Up ahead is the entrance to the Ribbon Cave,' Greg continued, shooing us on again. He tended to lag behind, rounding up stragglers and closing gates, before scurrying to the front of the group again. Sometimes, however, he got carried away, marching ahead until he reached the next set of switches. 'Mate of mine called Dan went up to the end of the Ribbon Cave, once, to change a light bulb,' he said. 'All the way up, Dan felt a breeze on the back of his neck. When he came to a halt, he heard the sound of a throat being cleared just behind him. Then someone grabbed his shoulder with very long fingers.' Pausing, Greg surveyed us, his eyes glittering. 'When Dan turned around, there was no one. Absolutely no one. He was alone in the cave.'

'All-*right*,' said Bethan, softly.

In the hush that followed, Michelle shivered. Gordon gave a sigh of satisfaction. Joyce nodded, smiling to herself.

Then Sylvia yelped.

'*Paul!*' she screeched. 'Don't *do* that!'

Most of us jumped, and stared.

38

'Scared ya,' Paul smirked.

'Yes, you certainly did,' said his mother, her hand to her heart. 'It's all right,' she gasped, smiling unsteadily at Richard. 'He grabbed my shoulder. It was a joke.'

Richard raised his eyebrows. Michelle and I exchanged glances. Mum whispered something to Ray.

Greg fixed Paul with an intent look, but didn't comment on his behaviour. Instead he remarked, still gazing at Paul, 'James Wiburd was supposed to have had very long fingernails. Because he liked digging in the mud.'

'Yes, that's all very well, but what about all these beautiful decorations?' Dad asked impatiently. 'How were they formed?'

Greg's face suddenly brightened. He immediately launched into a long geological lecture, which lasted about fifteen minutes as we slowly made our way out of the Orient and down towards the River Cave. We carefully descended several old metal ladders, using cable handrails. At the bottom we plunged into a network of round tunnels that Greg called the 'mud tunnels'. Some were so low that we had to bend over. There were holes in their roofs: little depressions like hoof-marks, or holes so large and long that you could see right through them to parts of the Orient Cave, just above.

'This is where we get most of our ghost sightings,' Greg announced. 'Here and around the corner near the Temple of Baal. There's a squeaky iron gate up here that sometimes closes by itself – *without squeaking*. And in the passage to the River Cave something interesting once happened to a guy in my tour group. Every single light bulb went out as he approached it, and turned on again as he passed.'

Everyone – even Paul – peered hopefully up at the electric lights over our heads. But nothing happened.

Richard, I noticed, had produced his electromagnetic field detector. He was studying it in a surreptitious way, as if he didn't want to make a big fuss.

'This place must be Elysium for ghost-hunters,' Joyce observed, smiling at Greg. For a moment he looked confused.

'Pardon?' he said.

'These caves. They must be heaven on earth. For people like us,' said Joyce, adjusting her glasses.

'Oh!' Something changed in Greg's expression. He began to nod. 'Oh, right. Heaven on earth. Elysium. Yes. Sorry – I got my wires crossed. There's a chamber in the Elder Caves called Elysium, you see. I thought that's what you were talking about.' Urging us forward, he continued to

talk, while we passed yet more wonderful formations: crocodile's teeth hanging from the ceiling,
petrified water spilling from a pot, plucked chick-
en's legs sticking up out of the ground. (I wish I
had written down more of the scientific names for
these things. Looking through my notes, I can only
find straws, flowstones, cave pearls and helictites.)
'As a matter of fact, we've been wondering if the
Elysium cave might be haunted,' Greg admitted.
'I haven't been there myself, because it's so hard to
get into; only a small person can squeeze through
all the tiny holes. But I've seen photographs. It's
one of the jewels of the caves. Not open to the
public, of course.'

'But why do you think it's haunted?' Richard
wanted to know, back behind me somewhere.

'Because a party of guides did visit it about six
months ago, and returned with a very strange story.'
Greg halted, so abruptly that Mum nearly ran into
him. 'See that needle-like formation, over there?' he
said. 'That's calcite which has crystallised on wire.
Scientifically it's very mysterious, because it forms
a lot faster than normal straws or helictites.'

'But what about Elysium?' Bethan wailed impatiently, and Rosemary giggled. Ray put a hand on
my brother's head.

Greg flashed a grin at him, before shooing us
down another passage.

'Well,' he said bringing up the rear, 'to begin with, while it's common for people to get stuck in the chute that leads up to Elysium, and to go sliding back down in a panic, it's *not* common to feel someone dragging you back by the ankles, as one of my friends did. What's more, when the party finally managed to squeeze their way into Elysium, the whole place was filled with a terrible smell.'

'Gas?' Dad suggested.

'Dead animal?' Richard proposed.

'Nup,' Greg replied. 'There were no carcasses. No piles of animal droppings. If it was gas . . . well, it's the first time we've ever encountered gas like that, in the caves. There can be too much carbon dioxide, sometimes, but nothing that sulphurous. Very strange.' He was squeezing past the rest of us, making for the head of the queue again. 'Now . . . just up ahead – those at the front can probably see – is the Pool of Reflections. I suppose you could call it a kind of lagoon belonging to the underground river, here, which we call the River Styx. Back in the old days, people used to row a boat across to the other side.'

I can't tell you how beautiful that pool was. It was quite long, and quite large, and it was as blue as toilet cleaner. Also, it was utterly, absolutely still – like a mirror. The reflections were so crisp that, if you had taken a photograph, and turned

42

the photograph upside down, you wouldn't have known which part was the reflection.

We all just stood and stared.

'This has to be a sacred place,' Matoaka breathed, and appealed to Greg. 'Is this a sacred site? Does it have an Aboriginal name?'

'Not as far as I know.'

'Then it must be invested with the power of the earth's own spirit,' said Matoaka, closing her eyes. She placed one finger on each temple.

Greg cleared his throat.

'Uh – yeah. Maybe,' he mumbled. 'Now every-body have a look down there, and tell me how deep you think the water is.'

We pressed against the railing, and stared down at the water. It was as clear as glass. At the bottom of the pool, I could see loose pebbles. There were no fish. No weeds. Nothing but pale stone.

'Is it about six feet deep?' Gordon hazarded. 'Eight feet?'

'It's sixty feet deep,' Greg replied, and we all gasped. 'Twenty metres. You couldn't tell, could you?'

'Amazing,' said Ray.

'If you were to drop something into that water,' Greg declared, waving us along the path that flanked the pool, 'any ripples created would take weeks to disappear.'

43

I don't know what made me glance at Paul, then. Perhaps the shuffle of shoes on cement. When I saw him digging around in his pocket, I knew *exactly* what he was going to do.

Fortunately, Ray was standing on the other side of Paul. And Ray must have reached the same conclusion as me.

'Don't even think about it,' he said quietly, his fingers closing on the back of Paul's neck. Then he nudged the stupid idiot forward, until the two of them were well past that tempting sheet of crystal-line water.

I heaved a great sigh of relief.

'We seem to get a lot of phantom tour groups, around here,' Greg informed us, as we left the Pool of Reflections behind. 'We've had maintenance guys hiding in the shadows to let a group pass, but the only thing that passes them are voices. No people. No lights. There's one guy called John who sings a lot while he's doing maintenance in here. He says he does it so he can't hear the ghosts.'

We clattered on, beneath the lowest arch in the Jenolan Caves, past old ladders that were once used as escape routes in case of floods. From the River Cave we took a detour through a cave called the Pool of Cerberus, where Greg pointed out the formation that had given the cavern its name. This formation looked rather like a dog's head. The second head was the shadow that it threw. The third head was its reflection, captured in the waters of the pool underneath it. 'A three-headed dog,' Greg explained. 'Like the monster that guarded the gates of the Underworld in Greek mythology.'

The Pool of Cerberus wasn't as big as the Pool of Reflections, but it was just as clear and still. A bridge had been thrown across it; according to Greg, a mysterious growling noise had occasionally been heard coming from beneath the bridge. Bethan wondered aloud if some kind of ancient monster was living there. Rosemary and Gordon took photographs, while Dad made loud suggestions about film stock and shutter speed. (He's a professional photographer. Did I ever tell you that?) Michelle's mum snuggled up to Sylvester. I asked Richard, in a low voice, if he'd picked up any readings on his electromagnetic field detector.

He gave a little shrug.

'There seems to be some ambient energy,' he replied, 'but nothing conclusive.'

'I still think there must be ghosts in here,' said Michelle, solemnly. 'There *must* be. It feels so *weird*. Don't you think?'

'I'm almost beginning to feel like a ghost myself,' Mum chimed in. 'I wouldn't be surprised if we came out and found that we'd been down here for two hundred years instead of two hours. It's got that feeling of timelessness.'

'That's not timelessness,' Dad corrected. 'You're mistaking timelessness for *geological* time. Geological time is on a different scale to the time that governs human existence.'

'Oh – well, excuse *me*,' my mother snapped.

And then Rosemary said, 'Where's Matoaka?'

CHAPTER # four

Everyone looked around. Sure enough, Matoaka wasn't with us.

Greg frowned.

'Who's Matoaka?' he demanded.

'My partner,' Dad replied, and Mum said, 'The one in the quilted Mexican jacket.'

'Okay. Fine.' Greg's voice suddenly changed. It wasn't light and pleasant any more. It was hard and serious. 'If you could all wait here – don't move – and I'll be back in a minute. Please don't move.'

'We won't,' Ray assured him, and Greg disappeared into the shadows.

There was a brief silence. I may be wrong, but I'm pretty sure that my mum was thinking unkind thoughts about Matoaka. (Something along the lines of: 'How typical of Jim to bring a total flake on a trip like this'.) You could tell she was impatient by the set of her jaw.

'*Oooo-ooo*,' said Paul, softly, making his ghost noise again.

'Oh, shut up,' said Michelle.

Sylvia opened her mouth, but before she could speak Rosemary interrupted – perhaps to prevent an argument. 'I hope your friend isn't lost,' she said to my dad.

'I'm sure she isn't,' Dad replied. 'The trouble with tours like this is that they're so tightly structured and inhibiting. You can't linger where you want to linger. You're surrounded by people – the magic gets lost –'

'Well, no one forced you to come,' my mother growled.

'So you think she's just lagged behind?' asked Richard, ignoring Mum, and Dad shrugged.

'Maybe a ghost got her,' Bethan suggested, with a trace of satisfaction. I gave him a nudge that meant 'shut up'. He's always saying the wrong thing at the wrong time. Not that you can blame him, mind; he's only eight, after all.

Paul Klineberg didn't have that excuse.

'Maybe she's fallen down a hole,' he said cheerfully. 'Maybe she drowned in the Pool of Reflections.'

Only someone who really wanted to be annoying would have made a comment like this. As long-suffering looks were exchanged around the group, I wondered – not for the first time – exactly what Paul was trying to do. Did he *want* someone to punch him in the face? Was he trying to make his mother angry?

If so, he didn't succeed. She just puckered her brow at him.

'Oh, Paul,' she remonstrated. 'Not now.'

'I might go and see what's happening,' Dad suddenly remarked. 'I might be able to help.'

'No,' said Ray. He sounded so firm, so blunt, that everyone looked at him in surprise. 'No, Greg told us to stay here,' he insisted. 'We should stay here.'

'Presumably he meant that we shouldn't go on,' was Dad's opinion. 'Doubling back won't hurt.'

'He told us not to move, Jim.' Mum's tone was sharp. 'What help are you going to be, anyway? You were never much help when we used to go camping.'

'Judy . . .' Ray put a hand on her arm. It was *so* embarrassing. I just wanted to disappear, like Matoaka.

Luckily, Paul was there to distract everyone's attention.

'Mum,' said Bethan. 'Paul just spat into the pool.'

After that, I didn't have to worry about Mum and Dad. They stopped arguing because they were too busy watching Richard scold Paul. I'd never seen Richard get angry before. He was quite impressive. He didn't shout or anything, but his face turned red. He's very tall, of course, and that certainly helped. So did the fact that he's so very articulate. After he had accused Paul of being puerile, boring, inadequate, disrespectful, narcissistic, maladjusted, vindictive and contentious, there wasn't much that Paul could say to defend himself – especially since he probably didn't understand half of the words that Richard had used. So he sulked instead.

Meanwhile, Sylvia apologised again and again. She tried to get Paul to apologise as well, but he wouldn't. Gordon and Joyce were politely examining a stalactite. Michelle's mum giggled into Sylvester's ear. (I could see why Michelle was cross with them; they weren't paying the slightest bit of attention to anyone except each other. Michelle might as well have been back at Caves House.) Rosemary checked her watch. Bethan yawned, showing everyone his tonsils.

I wondered what was keeping Greg. I could picture him wandering around the cascades of calcite, calling Matoaka's name. It occurred to me that if you *wanted* to hide in the caves, no one would ever find you. There were so many places to conceal yourself; I could imagine Matoaka crouched in a hollow somewhere. Falling asleep, perhaps. Falling asleep for a long, long time. For years and years. While the leaking walls slowly encased her in layer upon layer of ribbed and glittering stone, until she became just another one of those strange, unearthly formations . . .

I shook myself. Imagining things like that wouldn't help. It would simply make me nervous every time I was confronted by a large stalagmite. I'd be afraid that something might suddenly burst through the ice-like coating.

'Where have they got to?' Mum said uneasily. 'Surely she wasn't *that* far behind?'

'She's not on any kind of medication, is she?' Joyce asked Dad, who snapped, 'No! Of course not!' Then he started talking about the evils of psychiatric drugs. Meanwhile, Richard had finished with Paul. He was muttering something to Rosemary, his cheeks still flushed.

It was Sylvia who now hovered around her son, pleading with him in a low voice. Michelle, I noticed, was watching them both closely.

'What an idiot,' I murmured.

'Who?' said Michelle.

'Paul. Who else?'

'Do you reckon?' She narrowed her eyes. 'I think he's pretty smart.'

Before I could ask her what she meant by that, there was a yelp of relief from Gordon. Greg had reappeared. With him was Matoaka, who had a slightly hurt expression on her face. Greg's face was unreadable.

'Right,' he said. 'Problem solved.'

'What on earth happened?' asked Joyce.

Greg didn't reply. It was Matoaka who said, 'I couldn't move. The pool was calling to me.'

'You couldn't move?' Richard suddenly perked up. He turned away from his girlfriend, and rejoined the conversation. 'I've heard of that happening. People reach a certain point in the caves, and feel some kind of force pushing them back.'

'No, no.' Matoaka waved her hands dreamily. 'I was being called *forward*. Into the world of the spirit. Something was trying to communicate with me . . .'

'That was me,' said Greg, flatly. 'I was looking for you.' He gestured towards the stairs. 'If we could move on, now, we'll make our way out through the River and Lucas Caves.'

I think that Greg was a bit cross. He didn't really show it, but I got the feeling that he wasn't happy from the way he hustled us through the rest of the tour. There was no more talk about ghosts or séances; he only referred to things like the 8000-year-old bones of a brush-tailed rock wallaby, lying calcified in Lucas Cave, or the fact that cave explorers with a proper permit sometimes have to strip off and scrub themselves all over before entering a new cave, to ensure that they don't contaminate it with dust or dirt. He also mentioned that nineteenth-century visitors had often taken calcified bones away with them.

When we emerged into the Grand Arch, he informed us that the Jenolan Caves Trust didn't issue refunds in the event of the non-appearance of ghosts on the ghost tour. (Ha ha.) Then he asked us, politely, if there were any last questions.

Bethan put up his hand.

'Are there any tunnels that suddenly close up by themselves and totally disappear?' he inquired.

'Uh – no,' said Greg. 'Not unless there's a cave-in. And we carry out regular safety inspections, so –'

'Has anyone ever disappeared into the caves and never come out again?' Bethan interrupted.

'No. Never.'

'Not even an Aborigine?'

'Well – I mean, it's impossible to know exactly what might have happened before the Europeans arrived, though of course –'

'How do you know that the bones those visitors took away with them were animal bones and not human bones?'

'All right, Bethan, that's enough,' said Mum. She smiled apologetically at Greg. 'He's a bit over-tired.'

'I am *not!*'

'Bethan.' Ray put a hand on Bethan's head, and thanked our guide. 'It was wonderful,' he said. 'Very interesting. Very atmospheric.'

There was a murmur of agreement from everyone except Paul, who was moodily kicking at stones. Then Greg said goodbye. As the rest of us trudged back to the hotel, Michelle's mum proposed a quick drink before bedtime. She and Sylvester were walking along with their arms twined around each other's waists.

'Oh – I don't think so,' was Mum's response. 'It's very late. We've got to get these children to bed, I think.'

'*I'm* not tired,' said Bethan.

'Yes, you are,' said Mum. 'Thanks all the same, Colette.'

'I'm *very* tired,' Michelle announced. But if she was hoping that her mother would come upstairs, she was mistaken. Colette simply kissed her on the cheek and said, 'You've got the key, haven't you, my darling? You can sort yourself out – I'll be up very soon.'

Poor Michelle. She was furious, though she didn't show it much. Even Ray, I could see, cast her a troubled glance.

I've never been in love, myself, but it looked to me as if Michelle's mum was seriously in love. She didn't seem to care about anything . . . except Sylvester. And why she should have felt like that I don't know, because he really wasn't much. He was old, he had hairy hands, his teeth were full of fillings and he hardly said a word to anyone.

When we reached the Caves House foyer, everybody split up. Joyce and Gordon declared that they were ready for a hot bath, and made for their suite in the lodge behind the hotel. (They had paid extra for their own bathroom.) Richard and Rosemary joined Sylvester and Colette in the Explorers Bar. Matoaka decided that she was going to commune with the west wind, or something; I don't know exactly what she planned to do, but she disappeared into the night. So did Dad. Paul said he wanted to play snooker, and after a few quiet objections, Sylvia let him. Bethan wanted to play snooker too, but Mum's not like Sylvia. She put her foot down so hard that it practically went through the floor.

'No,' she stated. 'Come on. It's bedtime.'

Clumping up the stairs, I wondered what could have happened to Sylvia. During her two visits to our house she had been so cool, calm and collected. She had taken charge of the whole investigation, clicking around efficiently in high-heeled shoes.

And now she was letting her horrible son walk

all over her. It didn't make sense. Why was she being so nice to him?

Ahead of me, Mum and Ray were asking each other the same question, shaking their heads sadly. 'From what Trish tells me,' Mum was saying, in a very low voice, 'the ex-husband's a complete bastard. A total manipulator. Poor Sylvia's been fighting him every step of the way – the custody question has been a nightmare. This weekend's the first access she's had for over a month, because the husband's been so difficult. And of course Paul's been in the middle of it.'

'Even so,' Ray murmured, 'it won't do her any good to put up with that kind of behaviour.'

'I know. But the poor kid's testing her boundaries, Ray. He's looking for attention. It's so obvious.'

Ray sniffed. He's a very patient sort of person, but he has his limits. 'I'd give him attention, if he was mine.'

'It's an awkward age.' Mum whispered something (about me and Bethan, probably) whereupon Ray inclined his head.

I looked back at Michelle, who was mounting the stairs very slowly behind us.

'What did you think of the tour?' I queried.

'It was good,' she replied, without much enthusiasm. She seemed rather glum, and more than a little distracted. 'Pity we didn't see any ghosts.'

'Peter would have liked it, though. And Bettina. I wish they were here.'

'Yeah.'

'What did you think of all the ghost stories? Did they sound genuine to you?'

Michelle shrugged, but didn't reply.

'We might still see something,' I went on. 'Tonight, even. Since this hotel *is* supposed to be haunted.'

Michelle paused, one foot suspended above a stair. She peered up at me intently, opened her mouth, then shut it again. At the time, I couldn't understand why my words had had such an effect on her.

It only became obvious later, when I was in bed.

Getting to bed took quite a while. Firstly, I had to have a shower. (I always shower at night.) Then Matoaka wandered back from her evening yoga session – or whatever it was – and insisted on hanging dream-catchers above everyone's pillows. Ray had to slip downstairs and borrow a glass from the bar, so that Bethan could have water to drink during the night, if he needed it.

Then, after our lights had been turned off, Mum and Ray talked for a while, in very low voices that I couldn't hear properly. No doubt they were complaining to each other about Dad. After that, some people walked by our door, laughing. I could hear the plumbing in the bathroom as well.

But at last I started dropping off to sleep. My thoughts were just growing fuddled when someone began to pound on our door.

'Allie! Mrs Gebhardt!'

It was Michelle. Mum snapped on her bedside light. Ray sat up.

'Who's that?' he demanded. 'Michelle?'

'Let me in! Please!'

Ray threw back his covers, and went to let Michelle in. By that time, I was wide awake again; the only person who remained asleep in our room was Bethan. He could sleep through a hurricane.

'Michelle?' said Mum. 'What's the matter?'

Standing in the corridor, Michelle was wearing a shiny satin nightshirt that showed most of her skinny brown arms. She was hugging herself, as if she were cold.

'Something weird just happened,' she mumbled.

'Weird?' said Ray. I've never heard him sound so confused.

'In my room,' Michelle went on. 'It scared me.'

'What did?' I asked, but she wouldn't look in my direction. She was looking up at Ray.

'I turned off the light,' she gasped, 'and I was lying there, and someone *sat on my bed*! I could *feel* it! But when I turned on the light, no one was there!'

I knew instantly that she was lying. I mean, she's my best friend – she couldn't fool me. Though she was pretty convincing, I have to admit.

Ray scratched his head.

'Have you told your mother?' he inquired.

'I can't!' Michelle hunched her shoulders. 'She's not back yet!'

Ray looked at Mum, who pursed her lips. I had a feeling that Mum didn't believe Michelle, either. Possibly she'd drawn the same conclusion I had: that Michelle was telling stories so Colette would come back upstairs.

'Has your mother locked her door, Michelle?' Mum wanted to know.

'Yes.'

'So you can't move into her room?'

'No.'

Mum sighed. Ray said: 'Hang on. Just let me get changed.'

Ray was wearing his striped pyjamas. (He always wears the proper clothes in the proper place, unlike Mum. Mum wears an old crocheted poncho to bed, for some reason.) He pulled a pair of trousers over his pyjama shorts and replaced the striped top with a T-shirt. Then he padded out of the room in his bare feet.

After he'd gone, Michelle looked at Mum and said, defiantly, 'It did happen! It really did!'

'Perhaps you were dreaming,' Mum suggested, trying to be kind. But Michelle shook her head.

'I wasn't. I *know* I wasn't.'

'We'll probably all have nightmares, tonight,' Mum continued, rubbing her eyes. 'After that ghost tour. Aren't you cold in your nightshirt, Michelle?'

'No.'

'Are you sure? You'd better get in beside me. You *look* cold.'

'I'm not. I'm scared.'

Mum grunted. Michelle climbed in next to her, still avoiding my gaze. I probably would have been mad at her, if she hadn't been so upset. Her face was flushed, and she kept blinking a lot, as if she was blinking away tears. That's always a sign.

Then all of a sudden, Dad poked his head into our room.

'Is everything all right?' he asked.

He was wearing a lovely sort of white cotton dress, embroidered all around the collar and cuffs with coloured flowers and things. It must have been what he wore to bed. It was *very* pretty, though not what I would have expected to see on a man, somehow.

I suppose he and Mum have at least one thing in common, besides Bethan and me. They obviously aren't comfortable in normal, everyday pyjamas.

'Everything's fine,' Mum told him, sounding irritable. 'Michelle just had a bad dream.'

'It wasn't a bad dream, Mrs Gebhardt, truly!' Michelle insisted, using her earnest, library-monitor voice. 'It was a ghost, I'm sure it was!'

'A *ghost?*' said my father.

'On my bed! In my room!'

Dad clicked his tongue, and shook his head. 'You see, these are sensitive, intelligent kids,' he remarked, not exactly addressing Mum, but not really talking to himself, either. 'You can't feed them all this stuff without expecting a bad reaction.'

'Go back to bed, Jim,' Mum said coldly. 'It's under control.'

Dad sighed, and shook his head again. 'Good night, Alethea,' he said.

'Good night, Dad.'

He withdrew, and I heard his footsteps in the corridor. After that, there was a short lull. Michelle pulled Ray's bedclothes up under her chin. Mum yawned, and checked the clock on her bedside table. I made a face at Michelle, who made a face back at me.

Finally, her mum arrived.

'Michelle?' trilled Colette, appearing suddenly in the doorway. 'What's going on?'

Michelle looked up. 'There was a ghost,' she whimpered. 'In my room.'

'Oh, now that's just silly –'

'There was! I could feel it, sitting on my bed!'

'You were dreaming.'

'I was not!'

'Come.' Michelle's mum beckoned. Her bracelets jangled. Her lipstick was slightly smudged. 'Come out. Let these poor people sleep.'

'I'm not sleeping in that room again! I'm not!'

'You're not sleeping in here, either. Come.' As Michelle slowly pushed back Ray's covers and slouched across the floor, Colette turned to address Ray – who was hovering behind her. 'I'm sorry,' she said. 'I'm very sorry about this.'

Ray looked embarrassed. He waved a hand. Beside him, I could see Richard, who was bright-eyed and slightly red in the face.

'Where did it happen?' Richard asked. 'I could get my equipment . . .'

But someone shushed him. Rosemary, I think. She dragged him out of view, down the corridor. I could hear the murmur of their voices. Ray craned his neck to watch them go.

'Michelle seems a bit het up,' Mum remarked, from her nest of blankets. 'She needs to calm down, I think.'

'Yes, you're right.' Gently, Colette nudged her daughter out of the room. Michelle disappeared without a backward glance. I bet she was ashamed to look at me. 'It's been a big day,' Colette finished. 'A dramatic day. Good night, Judy.'

'Good night.'

'Thanks, Ray.'

'No problem,' Ray muttered. He waited until Colette was out of the way before re-entering our room. Even as he did so, I heard Michelle saying, 'Why doesn't Sylvester sleep in my bed, and I'll sleep with you? Sylvester doesn't believe in ghosts . . .'

Our door clicked shut. Ray rolled his eyes, and pulled his T-shirt over his head.

'Go to sleep, Allie,' said Mum. 'Show's over.'

'If there *was* a ghost,' I observed, doubtfully, 'we should probably report it to the people here . . .'

'I don't think there was a ghost,' said Mum. 'I think Michelle's suffering from an inflamed imagination.'

'Maybe.' I caught her eye. 'Still, though, it *might* be true.'

'Yes, it might be,' Mum sighed. She had seen what Eglantine could do. She had no reason to doubt the existence of ghosts.

'And if it is true, then the hotel should be told,' I pointed out. 'In case that room's haunted. Perhaps we should get Richard to check it with his electro-magnetic field detector.'

'Go to sleep, Allie,' said Mum.

'Even if it *was* just her imagination,' I went on, 'do you think anyone should sleep in there, until Richard's got a reading? I mean, you know what happened with Eglantine. You never let Bethan sleep in *his* room until Eglantine had gone.'

'*Go to sleep*, Allie!' It was Ray who spoke. He was back in his pyjamas, buttoning up his buttons. When he talks like that, you don't argue.

So I lay down and turned over. Bedsprings creaked as Ray got in beside Mum. 'Right,' he murmured. 'Let's hope that's it.' Mum switched off the light. There was a sigh in the darkness.

Then I heard a vague, sleepy voice.

Bethan's voice.

'Mum?' he yawned. 'Whass going on?'

CHAPTER # five

When I woke up, it was still dark. And I needed to go to the toilet.

The illuminated digits on my mother's bedside clock said that it was 2:12 a.m. I didn't really want to get out of bed at 2:12 a.m. I *especially* didn't want to leave our room. Richard had said that the lights were left on in all the Caves House corridors at night, to keep the ghosts away – but that didn't make me feel any better. On the contrary.

So I lay for a while, trying to ignore my bladder. It didn't work, though. In the end I was forced to get up, and creep across the floor, and cautiously pull the door open. Sure enough, lights were blazing in the corridor outside. It was as bright as day. This meant that I could only leave our door open a crack while I went to the bathroom. (I didn't want to get locked out, you see.)

Even though I tried to walk quietly, the floor creaked a bit. To reach the bathroom I had to turn my back on a very large window, which opened onto complete blackness. That was a bit scary. But everything else looked normal. It just didn't sound normal. It was unusually quiet.

There was no one else in the bathroom. All the shower stalls and toilet cubicles were empty. They smelled of chemical air freshener, which isn't a paranormal sort of smell. Even so, I was a bit nervous. Walking around in a strange place in the middle of the night always makes me nervous.

I remember wincing when I flushed the toilet. The gush of water sounded so loud that I was afraid it would wake up everyone on the floor. After that, I made a point of not using warm water when I washed my hands, because I knew what a terrible noise hot-water pipes could make.

Then, after passing through the little vestibule again, I tried to pull the bathroom door open.

It wouldn't budge.

At first I thought I must have locked myself in by mistake. So I didn't panic. It was only after I'd checked, and seen that there *was* no lock . . .

66

well, then I started to yank and push and kick and generally lose it.

'Come on,' I muttered. 'Come *on*. Hey! *Hey!* Is somebody out there?'

No reply. I banged on the door again, slamming it with both hands. I pulled and tugged at the handle.

'Hey!' I cried. *'Open up!'*

When nothing happened, I fell back, and looked around. It was a scary moment. The sweat was breaking out all over me, and my heart was pounding, and I was panting and squeaking and telling myself not to panic, the door was stuck, it didn't mean anything, I wouldn't be in there all night . . . that sort of thing. Leaving the entrance vestibule, I went back into the bathroom, looking for help. The only large object that wasn't fixed to the floor or wall, in that room, was the laundry basket, which was full of dirty towels. And I knew it wouldn't do me any good. The door was meant to open *inwards*. So I could pound on it all I wanted without making the slightest difference.

I approached the door again. I braced myself. I clenched my teeth and grasped the handle and *heaved* . . .

. . . and the door sprang open so smoothly, so easily, that I fell on my bum.

Whomp!

There was no one on the other side. I scrambled over the threshold before I was even on my feet, not wanting to risk being stuck inside again. I looked to the right: nothing. I looked to the left: nothing. It wasn't far to our room – just a few steps to the left, around a corner, and a few steps more, heading towards the window. But as I approached the corner, I began to slow down. I don't know why. Perhaps because I had this image in my head: an image of a face materialising out of the darkness on the other side of the window. I didn't want to turn the corner. I didn't want to see anything like that. It was stupid, I know. But I went slowly, very slowly, until I was at the corner . . .

'Boo!'

'*Aagh!*'

I almost died. I almost lay down and died on the spot. I fell against the wall, and Paul started to laugh.

He covered his mouth, but he was snorting and snickering.

'Scared ya!' he crowed.

I just stared at him. I couldn't believe it. He had jumped out in front of me.

'Did you think I was a ghost?' he grinned.

'What – what are you *doing?*'

'Who did you think was pulling the door?'

I looked around. I couldn't see Sylvia.

'Are you *crazy?*' I hissed.

'You should have seen your face!' He really seemed to expect that I would enjoy the joke too. 'What a great idea.'

'You're insane,' I said, getting angry. 'What are you doing, creeping around at this hour?'

'What are *you* doing?' he retorted.

'I'm going to the toilet.'

'Well – so am I.'

I didn't believe him. I was about to say so when the door nearest us suddenly opened, and a bleary, rumpled face peered out, crossly. The face didn't belong to anyone I knew.

'Do you *mind?*' (Whoever it was, he didn't appreciate being woken up.) 'There are people trying to sleep!'

'Sorry,' I murmured. Paul didn't say anything.

The head withdrew, and the door closed.

'You're such a jerk,' I whispered to Paul. If there's one thing I hate, it's being scolded by strangers. Especially for something that isn't my fault. 'You make me sick.'

Then I marched back to my room, before he could say anything else. I was *so* furious. It took me ages to get to sleep, because I kept thinking of things that I should have said to him. I also started wondering if I should tell Mum and Ray about it the next morning. Yes? No? If Paul got into trouble, would that spoil the tour? Would it create further tension?

In the end, I did tell Ray. I woke up very early, at a quarter to six, and saw him dressing in one corner. His shuffling and zipping had roused me. He was pulling on his shoes.

'What are you doing?' I whispered, and he looked up, startled.

'Oh.' He winced. 'I'm sorry, Allie. Was I making too much noise?'

'Where are you going?' I had noticed, suddenly, that his sketchbook, pencil box and water bottle were sitting on the floor near him. 'Are you going to draw?'

He nodded, and put a finger to his lips.

'I'm just going for a bit of a walk,' he said, in a very soft voice. 'See if I can find any interesting rock formations.'

'Please can I come?'

'Quietly.'

He waited for me outside the room. I put on my clothes as quickly and quietly as I could, remembering to take my hat. Mum always gets mad if we don't wear a hat in the sun.

Though I have to admit that it wasn't terribly sunny, just then. The sun had only just risen, and the valley was deep in shadow. Ray and I saw this as soon as we walked out of the foyer, and looked

70

around. We hadn't said much coming down the stairs. It was still very early, and we were frightened of disturbing people.

'Doesn't it smell good?' said Ray, drawing a deep breath through his nose. 'So clean.'

'Where are we going?'

'There's something called the Carlotta Arch walk. It starts over there.' Ray pointed across the road. 'It's supposed to contain "many panoramic views and geological features".'

'Can I please have a sip of your water?'

We crossed the road and began to climb the first set of stairs. It led us up a steep slope to a path that headed straight for the sky. This path was lined with lampposts and iron railings, and zigzagged up the side of the valley. On the way, it passed a bushland regeneration project, and a couple of wooden benches, and the peaked, red roofs of Caves House. As we climbed higher and higher, Caves House grew smaller behind us. I could see the road far below, disappearing into the Grand Arch. When I peered up, I was surprised to spot a tumble of rocky cliffs towering over us. They were streaked and cracked and full of strange, smooth holes, like a Swiss cheese.

A blue wren flitted by.

'Aren't we lucky?' said Ray. I don't know exactly what he was talking about (the weather, perhaps?), but he smiled at me, and I smiled back. Then I said, 'Paul nearly scared me to death, last night. He was pretending to be a ghost when I went to the toilet. At *two o'clock in the morning*.'

'Oh, dear.'

'He's such a jerk,' I went on. 'He pulled the door shut, and then he jumped out at me. He really likes scaring people.'

'You mean he was wandering around the hotel?'

'I don't know. He *said* he was going to the toilet.'

Ray sighed. He seemed to be thinking. We were both a bit out of breath at that stage, so we didn't say anything for a while. At last we reached a fork in the path, and Ray stopped. He looked at the sign pointing towards Lucas Rocks. Then he said, 'Let's not worry about Paul, just now. I'll have a word to Sylvia, but I don't know if it's going to help. He's a very troubled boy.'

'I wish he wasn't here.'

'Yes. Well. You won't get any argument from me.'

We turned left, and kept walking along the track, up and up. By this time we were high enough to catch the pale morning sun. There were white butterflies flitting about. Birds were chirping, and ants were scurrying, but we were the only people on the track. It felt as if we were the only people in the world. Overhead, the sky was a pearly colour. You could tell that it was going to be a beautiful day.

Then the path seemed to swerve, and suddenly we were looking through an enormous rocky arch, down at the shimmering blue water far below. The mouth of the arch was hung with grey stalactites. There was a viewing platform in front of it, and railings, and a sign.

'Wow,' sighed Ray.

We gazed for a while, soaking up the view, before Ray finally declared that he wanted to do a quick sketch of the stalactites. I said I'd wait. At first I stood behind him, watching the quick, clean strokes of his pencil. (He's very good, you know. I get a bit jealous sometimes.) But I have to admit that I didn't find the stalactites as interesting as Ray did. So eventually I drifted away, to inspect the big hole in the ground that lay opposite Carlotta Arch, on the other side of the track. It was a kind of crater, about four or five metres deep, and about as wide as two cars parked end to end. A fence stood in front of it. You could tell at first glance that it had been formed when the ground suddenly subsided. There were still bushes and vines growing on the bottom – or what looked like the bottom. But when I studied it more closely, I realised that the bottom of that hole wasn't *really* the bottom.

All along the edges, where the walls of the crater should have joined its floor, there was just dark, empty space. In other words, if you dropped into the hole, you could walk forward, duck your head, and squeeze into a cave that had been exposed to the air when the ground collapsed.

All at once, I remembered something. Greg had talked, the night before, about a 'sinkhole' entrance to the Elder Cave. You had to abseil down there, he'd said.

I wondered if this was the sinkhole. It certainly *looked* like a sinkhole. I was wondering what it would feel like to abseil down into the darkness, when I heard a rustling noise.

It wasn't the kind of rustle that's normally caused by the wind. It was a short, sharp, scrabbling rustle. Besides, there wasn't any wind.

I looked around, hoping to see a snake or a lizard. But nothing moved. Even Ray was motionless; he was staring at the arch, as if hypnotised. Disappointed, I turned back to the sinkhole.

There were butterflies flitting around down there. They made it look harmless. In fact I could see why people wanted to go exploring caves – there was something very tempting about that yawning rim of shadow. I felt a bit of an urge to wriggle in there and see what was concealed by the lip of rock, behind the ragged curtain of vines and dangling roots. But I couldn't, of course. There was a fence, and a locked gate. Not that they would necessarily have stopped anyone who really wanted to get in, but you could see that the sinkhole was off limits. Dangerous, probably. Unstable, perhaps. Not such a great place for hide-and-seek after all.

I wondered if any bushrangers had ever hidden in the Jenolan Caves. Then I wondered if anyone was hiding in them right at that very moment – an escaped prisoner, perhaps. Then I stared into the gaping blackness in front of me, and was overcome by a horrible feeling that someone *was* in there, beyond the reach of the sunlight, waiting and watching. It was the weirdest sensation. Particularly when my awareness shifted, and I became convinced that someone was *behind* me, practically breathing down my neck.

I turned with a gasp, just in time to see a low, dark shape scuttling into some thick bushes near Ray.

I gave a yelp.

'What?' said Ray, turning. 'What's wrong?'

'A wombat!'

'What?'

'I think I saw a wombat!'

'Where?'

'Over there!'

I showed him. The bushes weren't moving any more. I couldn't hear any suspicious noises, either. But when I reached the place where I'd last seen the scuttling shape, and poked around . . .

'Phew!' said Ray.

'Yuk.'

'Something must be dead.'

'But it was moving . . .'

The smell got worse the more I scrabbled around in the undergrowth. At first, it was like a very bad fart. Then it made me think of driving past a field recently fertilised with blood-and-bone. Finally, Ray began to cough.

'Aaugh,' he spluttered. 'This is – this is *awful*. Come away . . .'

'You can see where something's bent back the branches.'

'Come *away*, Allie!'

By this time I was holding my nose. It helped, but not much. I seemed to be actually *tasting* the smell, which was now as strong as a leaking gas tap. What's more, when we moved, we didn't leave it behind. I could have sworn that we were dragging it with us.

Ray, who's a bit asthmatic, was coughing like someone with pneumonia.

'Down there,' he gasped. 'You first.'

And he pushed me towards the closest stairs,

which coiled their way around Carlotta's Arch before zigzagging down a steep slope towards the Devil's Coach-house. A rugged wall of grey rock rose up on our right, pierced with dark, mysterious holes. Pale tree-trunks writhed against a dense backdrop of grey-green scrub. Everything was engulfed in shadow.

The stench was now so bad that I found myself taking quick, shallow little breaths. Perhaps that's why I was getting dizzy. Behind me, Ray was coughing his guts out. And then three things happened, almost simultaneously.

First of all, I slipped. What with the dizziness, and the stairs, and the way we were hurrying along, I lost my balance, sliding down several concrete steps. At the same time, Ray cried out, *'What the hell –?'* And before he could even finish his sentence, the sound of other voices reached our ears.

There were people climbing the path towards us. We couldn't see them, but we could hear them talking.

They were talking about someone called Phil, whose son was a drug addict.

'Ow,' I said. I had grazed my shin.

'Are you all right?' Ray panted.

'Yeah . . .'

'Did you hurt yourself?'

'A bit.' I was already on my feet again. What's

more, I was breathing normally. I *could* breathe normally. With a suspicious sniff, I realised that the bad smell was pretty much gone.

Suddenly, for some reason, it had disappeared.

'. . . so I told him, you can't live like that,' a woman's voice was saying. 'You've got to talk to someone, find out what your options are . . .' She stopped, abruptly, as we caught each other's eye. She had appeared at the bottom of our flight of stairs, emerging from behind a screen of bushes. I was standing at the top, on one leg.

Two other women in sensible boots soon joined her.

They smiled and nodded. Ray smiled and nodded. He and I edged to one side, so that they could pass us easily. As they did so, he said, 'Er . . . we struck a rather nasty smell, back there.'

The women stopped in their tracks. Three red and sweaty faces turned towards us.

'Pardon?' one of them said.

'There was an odd smell, up there. I don't know what it was . . .' Ray was speaking normally again, though he sounded a little embarrassed. 'Just thought I'd better warn you . . .'

'What kind of smell?' the oldest woman wanted to know.

Ray and I exchanged glances. What kind of a smell? It was hard to say.

'A strong one,' Ray finally replied.

The three ladies nodded, thoughtfully. They, too, exchanged glances. At last the leader said, 'I see. Well – thank you.'

'Thank you,' the other two chorused.

'We'll keep that in mind.'

And they marched on. I couldn't help wondering if we should have warned them not to go. But we waited for a couple of minutes, and heard nothing to worry us. Just the fading murmur of ordinary conversation.

'Are you all right?' Ray repeated.

I glanced up at him.

'That was weird,' I said, nervously.

'Yes.'

'What happened?'

'I don't know.'

'It was such a terrible smell . . .'

Ray grunted. He took my hand, and we began walking again. Stretches of concrete path alternated with flights of concrete stairs. We didn't stop to look at the yawning mouth of the Devil's Coach-house, but continued down to a dry and overgrown creek bed. Beneath a tunnel of arching branches, the path became a dirt track, lined with steel lamp posts.

'You don't think it was something dead, do you?' I remarked, trudging along. Ray was still holding my hand.

'Maybe,' he said.

'Do you think it *followed* us?'

'I don't know, Allie.'

'That's what it felt like.' I thought for a bit. 'Could it have had something to do with that animal I saw?'

Ray didn't reply. The path had swung around, and we were now heading straight into the Devil's Coach-house. Its barbed archway towered above us, black and forbidding. I wondered if there was any other route back to the hotel.

Probably not.

'Maybe we ought to tell someone,' I suggested.

'We will,' said Ray.

'Really?'

'Really.'

'Because it might be important.' I was struck by a sudden idea. 'Maybe there's gas coming out of the sinkhole! Remember what Greg said about that sinkhole? It leads to the Elysium Cave! And that's where all those guides smelled a funny smell!'

'We'll inform the appropriate people,' said Ray.

'As long as it wasn't Paul,' I muttered. 'It's the sort of thing he *would* do, if he could, but – I mean, he isn't smart enough. Do you think?'

No comment from Ray.

'Unless he brought a stink bomb with him,' I added, and glanced over my shoulder.

Behind us, the shady path was now dappled with sunlight. A soft breeze rustled the tightly packed branches. In the distance, a kookaburra cackled to itself, then fell silent.

I couldn't see anybody, or anything. But huge boulders lay in dense pools of shadow. Spiky thickets closed in on all sides. Beyond them, the rearing cliffs were full of holes and fissures.

How could I know, for a fact, that we weren't being followed?

CHAPTER # six

When Ray and I reached Caves House, we found our room empty. Mum and Bethan had already gone off to breakfast.

So we joined them downstairs.

There was a buffet laid out in the dining room. The way it worked was that you paid a fixed amount of money, and ate all you wanted. You had a choice of cereal (three kinds), stewed fruit (two kinds), fresh fruit, bacon, toast (three kinds) eggs, pancakes, coffee, tea and juice. My brother was in heaven.

'You can eat all you want!' he crowed, when I reached the chair that Mum had reserved for me. 'You can have anything you like!'

I have to admit, it *was* pretty exciting. I'd never eaten a buffet breakfast before. Usually, when we stay at motels, my family brings its own wholegrain bread and organic milk and homemade muesli.

This time, however, breakfast had been included in the price of the room.

Just in case you're wondering, I had Corn Flakes, stewed apricots, toast with Vegemite, two pancakes, a rasher of bacon and a spoonful of scrambled eggs. Bethan had *four* pancakes, a bowl of Nutri-grain, and lots of honey on his toast. Mum ate mostly fruit, and Ray mostly bacon.

Dad arrived – with Matoaka in tow – while I was still making my choice. He had brought some kind of wheat-germ/millet mixture in a plastic box. Having dumped some of this stuff into a cereal bowl, he doused it in hot water, and threw on a few pieces of fresh fruit. That was his breakfast.

To my surprise, Matoaka ate a lot of eggs. Obviously, she isn't one of those really *strict* vegetarians, like Mum's friend Trish. While she ate, she talked and talked, about auras and rebirthing and spirit guides. She talked so much that no one else got a word in edgewise, until Richard turned up.

He came straight over to our table, interrupting Matoaka's lecture on the medicinal qualities of honey. Rosemary was with him.

'Just thought I'd mention that there's another

ghost tour today,' he announced. 'I got talking to one of the bartenders last night, and he was very interested in PRISM. He wants to join, in fact. And he's been collecting information about Caves House, so he promised to give us a quick guided tour at eleven, before he starts work. We'll be meeting in the foyer.'

Dad clicked his tongue, eyes downcast. Bethan continued to stuff his mouth; I doubt he'd even heard. Mum said, 'I'm not sure what we'll be doing, yet, but we'll keep that in mind. Thanks, Richard.'

'His name's Jason,' Richard continued cheerfully. 'The bar-tender, I mean. He tells me that there was a mysterious incident last night in the guest lounge.'

'Really?' I pricked up my ears.

'Someone tried to use the computer this morning, and couldn't. The only thing that's coming up on the screen is "Hahahahahaha".'

Ray grunted.

'And there was a key left under the keyboard,' Richard added. 'One of those old-fashioned keys. Spooky, eh?' He put his arm around Rosemary. 'Though it was probably a prank.'

'It was probably Paul,' I corrected. Ray glanced at me sharply. Richard narrowed his eyes.

'What do you mean?' he asked.

'Oh, Paul tried to scare me last night. When I went to the toilet. He was pretending to be a ghost.'

There was a brief silence. Even Bethan looked up, keen to know more.

'What did he do?' my brother demanded eagerly.

'He was stupid. That's all.'

'How?'

'He jumped out at me, all right?' I said crossly, and Mum frowned.

'You know, that's just not on,' she complained. 'Someone ought to tell Sylvia.'

'What Paul needs is a proper cleansing.' Matoaka spoke through a mouthful of egg. 'I could do it myself, except that I didn't bring the right oils.'

'It's not a cleansing he needs,' said Richard, pushing his glasses up his nose. 'It's a good kick in the butt.'

'Paul's got issues, Richard,' Mum pointed out. 'We've got to remember that. All the same –'

'All the same, it's not acceptable.' Ray cleared his throat and – perhaps to change the subject – added, 'By the way, Richard, did your bartender say anything about bad smells?'

Everyone turned to stare at Ray, except me. I fixed my gaze on my plate.

'Bad smells?' Richard echoed.

85

'You know. The sort of thing that Greg was talking about last night.' Ray looked around at all the puzzled faces. 'It's just that Allie and I smelt something really fierce, this morning. We went for a walk up on the Carlotta Arch trail, and there was this *shocking* smell –'

'Right after I saw the animal,' was my contribution. 'I don't know what it was. A wombat, or something.'

'It put me in mind of what Greg told us. About the Elder Cave and its nasty smell. I wondered if your bartender bloke said anything else about that.'

Everyone looked at Richard, who took off his glasses, rubbed his eyes, and shook his head.

'No,' he replied, before putting his glasses back on. 'Not a word.'

'Ah.'

'Was it a gassy smell?' asked Mum.

'Not really.' Ray glanced at me. 'I don't know. Do you think so, Allie?'

I shrugged. 'It was the worst thing *I've* ever smelled.'

'Where did you smell it?' Dad inquired, and I explained about the sinkhole. Richard scratched his chin.

'The sinkhole. That's where our adventure tour is starting this afternoon. At one fifteen.' Noticing several confused expressions, he hurried to explain. 'Rosemary and I have decided to go on that abseiling tour of Elder Cave. The one Greg mentioned. It starts at one fifteen, if anyone else wants to join us.'

Ray did. I couldn't believe it, but he did. Bethan did too, but Richard explained gently that the minimum age for the tour was ten years old. This, of course, meant that *I* was allowed to go. But I didn't want to. I'm not an abseiling sort of person.

Besides, Mum wasn't keen. She didn't want to go herself, and she *certainly* didn't want me taking part. In fact she wasn't very happy about Ray's involvement, either. Especially in light of what we'd been told about Elysium.

'Are you sure it's safe?' She addressed him in a low voice, but I could still hear her. 'I mean, we were just discussing that smell. Suppose it's gas, leaking out of the sinkhole? Do you think you should risk it?'

'Not without informing the appropriate people,' Ray assured her. 'Don't worry, I'll have a word with one of the guides. Right after breakfast.'

'Really? The smell was that bad?'

'Oh, yes.'

'Gordon and Joyce aren't going on the adventure tour,' Richard suddenly declared. 'They say they're too old. But Joyce has offered to lead a bushwalk with the people who don't go. She used to belong to the Wildlife Rescue Service, so she knows a bit about flora and fauna.'

At that moment, Sylvia Klineberg appeared at his side. She was neatly dressed in a crisp yellow T-shirt and cotton pants, but she looked pale and tired. Paul wasn't with her, I noticed.

When Richard asked her about the adventure tour, she blinked, and wrinkled her brow.

'Oh, I – I don't know,' she replied, sounding harassed. 'I have to make sure I get Paul back in time. He's a late riser – he's asleep at the moment . . .' (Ray and I exchanged glances.) '. . . so I think I'd better leave this afternoon clear, just in case.'

'Did you know that he was up late last night?' said Mum, before Ray could stop her. 'Allie went to the toilet, and he scared her to death, poor thing.'

Sylvia seemed confused. 'You mean – Paul was in the Ladies?' she murmured.

'No, no. He was creeping about, for some reason. I don't know why.'

'Oh, dear.' Sylvia rubbed her forehead. 'He doesn't sleep very well. We've been to the doctor about it. She thinks it's stress-related, but he won't do yoga, and sleeping pills are quite problematic, at his age . . .'

She looked so worried that Mum seemed to lose heart. Nothing more was said on the subject of Paul's crazy behaviour, though Matoaka recommended some kind of relaxing herbal tonic. Meanwhile, there was a flurry of movement. Richard suddenly decided that he was hungry, and headed for the buffet. Dad announced that it was time for his morning meditation. Michelle and her family entered the dining room, choosing a table that wasn't far from ours; Michelle waved at me, and I waved back at her.

Rosemary went to join Richard, who was hovering over the stewed fruits. But she hesitated as she passed my chair.

'Allie,' she said, 'how big was that animal you saw? The one near the sinkhole?'

I gazed up at her, and swallowed a slice of pancake before replying.

'I don't know. Big. Ish.'

'As big as a kangaroo?'

'Maybe. I didn't get much of a look. Why?'

'Oh – nothing.'

She smiled, and was about to go when something occurred to me.

'Did you have that dream last night?' I asked. 'The one about your grandmother?'

'No,' she said, looking a bit embarrassed. 'Why?'

'Just wondered.' I shrugged. 'She might not be able to follow you around. Where do you live, anyway?'

Rosemary hesitated. She had a funny look on her face, as if she couldn't believe that she was even discussing the subject.

'At the moment, I live with my mum,' she replied at last.

'In your old house? Where you grew up?'

'Well – yes.'

'That's it, then.' The more I heard, the more I was convinced that Rosemary had been seeing her grandmother's ghost. 'She wouldn't know where to find you anywhere else,' I explained. 'Your grandmother, I mean. If it was all in your head, it would be happening here as well.'

As far as I was concerned, the whole thing seemed perfectly obvious. Even Rosemary had to see the logic in what I was saying. And she did, I think. She blinked, and scratched her cheek. But she didn't smile.

'Yeah,' she murmured. 'Well . . . maybe.'

Then she wandered away towards the stewed fruits. Sylvia followed her. Matoaka suddenly realised that Dad was heading for the door, and jumped up, wiping her mouth. 'If I miss my meditation, I'll be constipated all day,' she informed us, before departing.

All at once, my family was on its own again.

'I want to do the ghost tour,' said Bethan, turning to look at Ray, 'but I want to play snooker first.'

Ray grimaced.

'You promised,' Bethan reminded him.

'I know, I know. I promised. I'll do it.'

'And I want to have a massage,' said Mum. 'Colette had a massage and she said it was fabulous. Expensive, but fabulous. I'll get my exercise this afternoon, when I do the bushwalk. But right now I want a massage.'

'Which leaves Allie,' said Ray. 'What do *you* want to do, Allie? Before the ghost tour, I mean. Presumably you want to do *that*.'

I glanced over at Michelle. She had already visited the buffet bar, and was now back at her table, sitting alone with a glass of juice and one slice of toast. Sylvester was on his feet, peering suspiciously at the stewed prunes. Colette was next to him, questioning a waitress about the milk. (Was it really skim, or just low fat?)

'It depends on what Michelle's doing,' I muttered.

'Go and ask her.' Mum stabbed at a slice of rockmelon. 'Maybe you two can just hang out for a while.'

Hang out. I hate it when Mum tries to sound trendy. I don't even know why she bothers, not

91

with me; some people just aren't trendy, and I'm one of them. In fact I've resigned myself to the fact. I'm brainy, not trendy.

'Okay,' I said, and crossed the room to where Michelle was sitting. She gave me a half-hearted smile. She had big dark circles under her eyes.

'Hiya,' she said.

'Is that all you're eating? Haven't you seen the fruit, and the eggs?'

Michelle sniffed. She's a bit of a connoisseur when it comes to breakfast buffets, because her mum loves posh hotels. 'They don't have any brioche,' she said. '*Or* any mushrooms.'

'Well, that's good, isn't it?' I glanced over my shoulder. 'It'll give Sylvester something else to complain about.'

This time, Michelle smiled a proper smile. Suddenly her mood seemed to improve. She told me that she had slept in her mother's room the night before, on a rollaway bed. Sylvester had been so angry about this that he'd slept in Michelle's room, just to 'prove there were no ghosts'. I shook my head, wondering why Michelle bothered to waste so much energy on getting back at Sylvester. Didn't she know how lucky she was, not sharing with Bethan? I would have *loved* my own room.

'So what happened?' I asked. 'Did Sylvester see any ghosts?'

'No.'

'Did *you* see any ghosts?'

Michelle flashed me a mischievous look, and sucked at her straw. When she didn't reply, I began to tell her that *I* had seen something – and smelled it, too. But I was interrupted by her mother.

'Allie.' Colette pulled out the chair next to mine. On the plate in her hand lay a single slice of rockmelon. 'How are you this morning?'

'Good. Thanks.'

'Do you have anything planned?'

'Well, as a matter of fact . . .' I explained about the eleven o'clock ghost tour. 'Did Richard tell you?'

'We discussed it last night,' Colette replied. 'I don't think it's a good idea. Not for Michelle.'

Michelle sat up straight, her eyes widening in alarm.

'Mum!' she protested. 'I've *got* to go! I'm in the Exorcists' Club!'

'Ghosts upset you, Michelle.' Colette carefully cut up her slice of rockmelon with a knife and fork. 'From what I could see, you weren't very keen on them last night. You can't have it both ways, I'm afraid.'

Michelle opened her mouth, then shut it again. She looked furious, but she couldn't think of a convincing argument. Her mother had her cornered.

'Besides,' Colette continued, 'this morning we'll be visiting another cave. One we haven't seen before. Something on the north side of the Grand Arch.' Chewing very slowly, she added, 'You can come too, Allie, if you want.'

Poor Michelle. She'd been a bit too clever for her own good. I would have gone with her, but I couldn't. By the time we had all finished breakfast, and checked with the guides' office, the only available north-side cave tour was scheduled for ten o'clock. Since it was going to be ninety minutes long, I couldn't join it without missing my exploration of Caves House.

All I could do was stay with Michelle as she waited in the Grand Arch. I felt even sorrier for her when I saw that Paul and Sylvia had bought tickets for the same tour of the Imperial Cave. They wandered up with about three minutes to spare. 'I would have liked to do the ghost tour, but Paul wanted to do this,' Sylvia explained to Colette. It occurred to me that Paul's interest in the Imperial Cave tour was almost certainly the result of a desire to stop his mother from doing anything else.

When he pulled a face at me, I scowled back at him.

'He's such a pain,' I said to Michelle.

'Sylvester's worse,' she replied.

'He can't be.'

'He is.'

'There's no comparison,' I protested, and Michelle suddenly gasped, as if struck by a sudden idea. I couldn't ask her what it was, though, because at that moment she was summoned by her tour guide. So I said, 'Good luck,' and wandered back to Caves House.

That was when I started writing this report. I got my notebook, and a pen, and I sat in the guest lounge, feeling important. There were a lot of visitors milling around outside, you see, but only people actually staying at the hotel were allowed to use the lounge. To my surprise, there was a big bowl of fruit on one of the tables – fruit that you could eat, if you were a guest – and magazines to read, and even a small library of books. For a while I was distracted by the marble statues dotted about, and by the flower arrangements, and the television. But at last I settled down to think about my report.

There was one thing puzzling me. In my experience, ghosts only seem to hang about when they desperately need something. Eglantine, for example, was desperate to finish her story. When we helped her to do that, she disappeared. Abel Harrow, the miner's ghost, was desperate to find gold. Poor little Eloise, the baby's ghost, was desperate for her mother. Once their needs were satisfied, there was no reason for them to stay.

So why were all these other ghosts hanging around the Jenolan Caves? Were *they* in desperate need of something? And if not, why were they trapped? Why did Miss Chisolm keep setting the same old dining-room table? Why did James Wiburd feel compelled to keep wandering round and round the same underground passages? It was as if they were stuck in a groove, unable to free themselves without someone else's intervention.

I was wondering whether James Wiburd's ghost might be guarding the caves, or protecting them, when Rosemary strolled in. She had been passing through reception, she said, and had seen me through the door. Flinging herself into one of the big, comfy chairs, she asked me what I was doing.

'Oh – writing about this trip,' I replied. 'Some of my friends couldn't come. They'll want to know what it was like.'

Rosemary nodded. She glanced towards the foyer. Then she leaned forward and said, 'I've been thinking about what you said. About my dream.'

I waited. She smiled awkwardly, scratching her nose.

'This is all new territory, for me,' she added. 'Ghosts and things.' She sort of giggled, adjusting her glasses. 'I was never particularly convinced, until I met Richard . . . he's told me some amazing things. About you, for example. Your house.'

I shrugged. 'It was haunted, but we got rid of the ghost,' I said.

'Exactly. You're a bit of an expert. So perhaps you're right. It's not *absolutely* impossible. What if my grandmother really *is* trying to tell me something?'

'You could always ask.'

'I have,' she admitted, surprising me a lot.

'You have?'

'What I mean is, when she first appeared – well, I more or less asked her what was wrong. I think.' Rosemary hesitated. 'I told Richard, but he never suggested she might be a ghost. I'm sure it never occurred to him.'

'Oh, well. Richard doesn't believe anything much, unless he's got a reading on his equipment,' I said, waving the subject of Richard aside. 'So what did your grandmother tell you?'

'Nothing. Not a thing. All she ever says is, *"I don't know what's going on! I don't know what's going on!"* Rosemary sighed. 'Nothing else.'

'Oh.' This didn't explain much. I wanted to help Rosemary, but how could I? What could her grandmother possibly mean? 'Do you think maybe she doesn't *know* she's dead?' I asked, and suddenly felt awful. Because Rosemary gasped. Tears filled her eyes. I had really upset her.

'It's probably not that,' I said quickly. 'She must know, after all this time. She'd have to be stupid not to.'

Rosemary cleared her throat, looking away. There was a brief pause. Then she remarked, as if wanting to change the subject, 'By the way, I've been thinking about that animal you saw. And the smell you smelled.'

'Really?' I was surprised.

'Of course, when I was researching the traditional beliefs of the Gundungurra tribe, I didn't really . . . well, you know. I'm not Aboriginal myself. And it all sounded pretty far-fetched.' She smiled a watery kind of smile. 'Though now, after all this talk about ghosts . . . well, it just sheds a different light on things.'

'What things? What do you mean?'

I was completely lost. Rosemary apologised. She explained that she had a theory – a theory about what Ray and I might have encountered, on our morning walk. Though it sounded ridiculous, it was probably worth mentioning.

'There's something in the Gundungurra mythology that fits,' she said. 'A monster called Mumuga, which had very short arms and legs, and hair all over its body. Mumuga couldn't run fast, but when chasing members of the tribe it used to make them sick and weak by moving its bowels all the time as it ran, so that its prey would be overcome by the stench, and fall down. That's how it used to catch them.' As I stared at her in amazement, Rosemary continued. 'I don't remember much else about it, but I do remember the business with the smell. After all, it's not easy to forget.'

'You mean – you think a Mumuga was trying to catch us? Me and Ray?'

Rosemary's smile this time was firmer. 'Not exactly. I mean, I don't necessarily *believe* that's what happened. I'm just passing along some information. Because it seems relevant.'

'Oh.'

She glanced at her watch, and rose from her chair.

'Well, I guess I'd better go and find Richard,' she said.

'Wait – hang on –' I was still trying to sort out what she'd just told me. 'Has anyone else ever seen this thing? Or smelled anything anywhere?'

'I'm sorry, Allie, I wouldn't know.' She really *did* sound sorry. 'I'm no expert. These little mysteries – well, who can say? People talk about seeing yowies and bunyips and other strange spirit creatures, but there's never any proof. Perhaps you should try the Internet.'

99

I nodded, thinking furiously. The animal I'd seen – what had it really looked like? I'd had an impression of grey fur, and scuttling legs. Scuttling, *short* legs. But it had moved so quickly. (Too quickly for a Mumuga?)

'Anyway, I might mention all this to Jason,' Rosemary remarked. 'It's probably worth passing on to the staff here, you never know. Are you going to be joining Jason's tour, Allie? The ghost tour?'

'Oh – uh – yes.'

'Okay, I'll see you then. And . . . thanks for the advice.'

She left without mentioning her grandmother again. For a while after she'd gone, I tried to concentrate on my report, but I couldn't. So I finally went up to find Ray. I knew that he was almost certainly playing snooker with Bethan, on the first floor.

What I *didn't* realise was that Dad had decided to play too. When I walked in on them all, Dad was stretched across the pool table, working a cue through his fingers. Matoaka was watching him from a corner of the room. There were cans of soft drink scattered about.

'Did you buy lemonade?' I demanded, of no one in particular.

'There's one for you,' Ray quickly assured me.

'Come and sit here.' Matoaka patted the seat next to her, dimpling in my direction. 'You can tell me what you've been doing.'

'As a matter of fact, I've been talking to Rosemary.' But I was addressing Ray, not Matoaka. 'Do you know that the Aborigines around here used to be afraid of something called the Mumuga?' I informed him. 'It used to run after people, pooing all the way, so that the awful smell made them pass out and fall over.' As Ray lifted his eyebrows I added, 'It was small and hairy, with short legs. Just like the animal *I* saw.'

Ray blinked. Bethan frowned.

'You mean there's some kind of animal that *poos* people to death?' my brother demanded. 'That's *stupid*!'

'It's not an animal,' I said. 'It's – well, I don't know what it is exactly. A sort of spirit creature. Like a bunyip.'

Bethan snorted.

'You couldn't have seen a bunyip. There's no such thing.'

'How do you know?' I retorted. 'Lots of people reckon there's no such thing as a ghost! And we know *they're* wrong.'

'Well, I think it's stupid,' Bethan scowled, as Dad finally tapped a red ball with his cue. It bounced off a few other balls before trickling to a standstill.

'If I had been allowed to *concentrate*,' Dad said crossly, 'that might have been a better shot.' But Matoaka waved him down.

She was interested in what I'd been saying.

'Wait a minute, wait a minute,' she exclaimed. 'Allie, where did you hear this? From whom?'

'From Rosemary.'

'And she told you *what*?'

Patiently, I repeated myself. Matoaka got very excited. While Bethan stubbornly wielded his cue (which, though short, was still too long for his arms), Matoaka began to crow and gasp over my news.

'I had a feeling!' she insisted. 'I could *sense* something, from the moment I arrived. Didn't I tell you, Jim? I knew this place was spiritually significant.'

'But it might *not* have been a Mumuga,' I pointed out. 'Rosemary just mentioned it, because she liked the coincidence.'

'Oh, of course it was a Mumuga, Allie, what else could it have been?' said Matoaka. 'What else would make a stink like that?'

'A broken sewage pipe.' Ray spoke softly, from the edges of the conversation. 'A dead animal. A gas leak.'

'Yes, and anyway, if this stench was a hunting technique, then why has no one else been attacked, around here?' Dad wasn't convinced. 'I mean, apart from the stink in the caves, where else has this alleged creature cropped up? Why attack Ray and Alethea, and no one else? It doesn't make sense.'

It didn't, either. Matoaka opened her mouth, but nothing emerged; she was trying to think of an answer. Bethan gave his target ball a huge *whack*, and sent it bouncing off the table.

Ray cleared his throat.

'Ah . . . it's just a thought,' he said, 'but – well, it *does* make sense, in a funny sort of way. If you consider that I have some Aboriginal blood in my veins.'

CHAPTER # seven

The ghost tour was kind of spoiled for me, after that.

Not that it wasn't good, or anything. The bartender, Jason, was a very funny guy. He was young and fair, with a round, plump face; he told us all kinds of amusing stories about guests who got lost in Caves House, and guests who wanted furniture rearranged because they were hooked on Feng Shui, and guests who came thousands of miles just to spend all their time in the bar, and one guest who insisted that he'd seen a ghost, even though the ghost was a housekeeper. (This guest, apparently, hadn't been taking his medicine.)

Jason also told us some pretty good ghost stories.

He started in the dining room, where he described how, one night, some staff locked the doors after the guests had left. In those days, a chain was always stretched through the door handles, to prevent anyone getting in before morning. As the staff watched in dismay, the heavy doors strained against this chain, as if someone was trying to open them from the inside.

'Of course, that was a long time ago,' Jason said. 'More recently, during renovations that took place about six or seven years ago, the painters had a lot of trouble with ghosts. One of them was working on a scaffold when he looked around and saw a lady dressed in nineteenth-century clothes. He called out to his mates, and they turned just in time to see her fading away.'

According to Jason, the same poor painters had stored their supplies in Room 123 – Miss Chisolm's room. They tended to leave their stuff scattered about untidily. But then one night some nearby guests heard a lot of noise coming from that room, though they saw no one entering or leaving it; the next morning, when the painters arrived at work, they found that their paint cans had been neatly arranged against one wall, from the smallest to the largest, and that their other equipment had also been tidied up.

'It could have been Miss Chisolm,' Jason said,

with a grin. 'On the other hand, it could have been a few of the staff, dropping a hint. No one will admit to it, either way.'

Jason actually showed us Room 123, and Room 104, too. There was nothing very special about either of them. Richard searched in vain for interesting energy signatures, while Bethan closely examined the walls (hoping, no doubt, to see evidence of paranormal scribbling, like the scrawls that kept turning up in his bedroom before we got rid of Eglantine). Meanwhile, I was distracted by some unanswered questions that I kept turning over and over in my mind. One of them involved the ghost dog in the car park. Had it really been a ghost, or had it been the Mumuga? And what about all those other strange experiences in the caves: the growls under the bridge, the closing gates, the vanishing figures? What if *they* had been the Mumuga, as well? What if Dad had been right after all? I remembered what he had said, the day before: *'This land is of great importance, but not because of any ghosts. Its transcendental quality is derived from its place in Aboriginal spirituality.'*

Maybe we should have listened to him, I thought.

It was a pity that these questions were bothering me, because it meant that I couldn't really enjoy Jason's stories. I was also preoccupied by Ray's astonishing news. I couldn't *believe* that he was part Aboriginal. He'd never said anything about it – not to me, not to Bethan, not even to Mum. She was as amazed as the rest of us, when she turned up after her massage. Ray explained that the connection was pretty tenuous; his great-great-grandmother, he said, had been Gundungurra, from around Lake George. But Ray had never known her, or known anything much about her, except that her name was Fanny Russell.

All the same, Matoaka kept trying to find out more. Whenever Jason wasn't talking – whenever he was clambering up stairs in front of us, or sifting through his bundle of keys – Matoaka would sidle up to Ray and press him for details. What was Ray's totem? Where were his ancestors buried? Had his choice of profession been influenced by any 'deep-seated spiritual yearning towards the land'?

Ray kept saying 'I don't know', while Dad looked crosser and crosser. Perhaps he didn't like the fact that his girlfriend was suddenly so fascinated by Mum's boyfriend. Actually, I don't know why Dad had decided to come along in the first place. He'd made it pretty clear what he thought about ghosts, and the people who chased them.

He probably just didn't want to be left out.

Anyway, what with Matoaka whispering in the background, and Dad's impatient snorts, and

Bethan's stupid questions ('Do you ever get tables floating around, or anything?') . . . what with all that, I didn't get as much out of the ghost tour as I should have. Especially since I found myself missing great chunks of what Jason said, because my mind had wandered to the question of how you could actually track down a Mumuga. That's why this section of my report, on the tour of Caves House, isn't very thorough. I'm really sorry about that. I wish I'd paid more attention. I wish I hadn't been so distracted.

However, let me assure you that it could have been a *lot* worse – if I'd gone with Michelle, for instance. I found this out after Jason had left. Those of us who'd taken part in his tour were all standing around in the corridor outside our rooms, talking about lunch, when we heard heavy footsteps approaching: *bang, bang, bang!* All at once Michelle appeared, rushing along. I was too far away to reach her – she unlocked her door and slammed into her room without even looking around – but I could see that she was *very* upset. Within seconds, the sound of Colette's voice reached us (*'Michelle! Michelle!'*). Next thing we knew, Michelle's mother was rattling Michelle's door, trying to get in.

'Open up, please, we have to talk,' she said. 'Michelle? Come on, now.'

Mum gave me a prod. Looking up, I saw her jerk her chin at me.

'Come on,' she murmured.

'Huh?'

'We're going to lunch. Bethan? Lunch.'

'But Mum –'

'*Lunch*, Allie. *Now*.'

As we moved, Colette must have seen us out of the corner of her eye. She stopped knocking.

'Is there another key?' she demanded, her face all drawn and tight. 'There must be another key.'

The rest of us exchanged glances. Richard, who was slightly flushed, pushed his glasses up his nose and said, 'At reception, perhaps?'

'Please could you get it? Could you ask someone? I can't get in.'

Of course I didn't want to go. I wanted to ask about Michelle: what was wrong with her? What had happened? Mum, however, wouldn't let me stay. She took hold of my wrist and marched me downstairs to the bistro. No matter how much I protested, she wouldn't give me a chance to find out what was going on. 'It's a family thing,' she insisted. 'It's between Michelle and her mother. We have to leave them alone.'

'But what if I can help?'

'If they want help, they'll ask for it. Now come

and decide what you'd like for lunch. A nice roll, perhaps?'

In the bistro we met up with Sylvia, who was standing in line at one of the counters. Poor Sylvia looked close to tears – even a little angry. But she wasn't angry at Paul.

'Such a silly episode,' she fretted. 'It absolutely *ruined* the whole tour. I have to say, I don't think much of the way certain people behave, I really don't.'

'Why?' asked Mum, in astonishment. 'What happened?'

'Oh, I don't know.' Sylvia glanced at her watch; the line was moving very slowly. 'That Mrs du Moulin must have some serious *issues*, as far as I'm concerned. She's a grown woman, for God's sake, what's she afraid of?'

After a lot of careful questioning by Mum, Sylvia revealed the source of the problem. Michelle, she said, had been getting friendly with Paul on the cave tour. They had been chatting and laughing and having fun. For some strange reason, Colette had disapproved.

'Can you believe it?' Sylvia complained. 'I mean, *obviously* an adolescent sense of humour isn't everyone's cup of tea, but there's no point losing your temper. You'll only make things worse.'

Mum and I were very careful not to look at each

other, though I noticed that Ray shifted uncomfortably. I'm pretty sure we all had a good idea of what Paul's 'adolescent sense of humour' must have been like. Jumping out at people, spitting into pools, pissing on formations . . . it could have been anything. And Michelle had laughed! That was what I found very strange.

Until Sylvia went on.

'So then Michelle and her mother had a shouting match – it was terribly embarrassing – because the poor girl has evidently been forced to put up with all her mother's various *men* . . .' At last Sylvia reached the counter, and ordered a serving of hot chips. 'All that noise, in such a confined space . . . it was really dreadful. The guide had to get quite firm.'

Suddenly I understood. Michelle had been trying to make a point about Sylvester. She had used Paul to get back at her mum. (If Colette could object to Paul, why couldn't Michelle object to Sylvester?) It was smart, I suppose – but *I* wouldn't have done it.

I don't think.

'So where is Paul now?' Ray inquired.

'Oh, he went straight upstairs, poor thing. He was quite disturbed.' Sylvia paid for her chips. 'I'm taking these up to him now. Then I think we might hit the road. Could you tell Richard, for me? I don't want to be late getting Paul back to his father.'

111

Mum and Ray agreed to pass the word to Richard. After which, having said goodbye to Sylvia, they took me over to the table that Bethan had already chosen. My brother wanted a hamburger for lunch, but Mum wouldn't let him have it. She bought us each a ham salad roll, and made us split a serving of chips between us. At first, we didn't talk much. Bethan was too busy trying to finish his roll quickly, so that he could get stuck into the chips before me. I was mulling over Michelle, wondering what I could do to help. So were Mum and Ray, I think. They were certainly mulling over *something*.

At last Dad turned up, with Matoaka. Richard, they told us, had fetched the extra key to Michelle's room. Colette had gone in and shut the door. No doubt, Dad said, she and Michelle were now sorting things out together. 'Merging families,' he added, 'can be a very difficult thing. Absorbing an outside personality can really destabilise relationship patterns.'

Mum looked up sharply. My heart sank, because I knew exactly what she thought: she thought that Dad was having a dig at Ray. I couldn't tell you whether he was or not, but Mum always assumes the worst, with Dad. It's probably a bit unfair.

Fortunately, Ray jumped in before Mum could speak.

'I went to the guides' office this morning,' he informed her, 'and reported that smell. After you went off to your massage, Judy.'

'And?' said Mum.

'They told me they'd look into it.'

'Do you think they will?'

'Oh, I think so. They seem like a fairly professional bunch.'

'Did you mention the Mumuga?' Matoaka wanted to know. It was a stupid question. Ray pointed out that he hadn't known about any Mumuga, at the time. Matoaka urged him to go back, and tell the guides what Rosemary had told him.

'If you have Gundungurra blood, then the Mumuga might have responded to that,' Matoaka suggested, in her high, excited voice. 'It could have sensed that you were its traditional prey. Perhaps it *only* bothers people of your tribe, Ray, which would account for the way we haven't heard about anyone else encountering the same manifestation.'

'Except those guides in Elysium,' I interjected, whereupon Mum leaned over and said: 'Eat up, Allie. We're all waiting for you.' I got the feeling that she was trying to ignore Matoaka.

But Ray frowned.

'You know,' he said, hesitantly, 'the funny thing is . . . well, I didn't mention it before, because I

113

thought it was probably a branch, or something, but . . . to tell you the truth, something did catch me around the leg, while I was going down the stairs. Just before you tripped, Allie, remember?'

I did.

'You shouted,' I remarked, with my mouth full of chips.

'Yes.' Ray gave an apologetic smile. 'In the context of what Rosemary told us, I suppose it *was* a bit strange . . .'

'Are you finished, Allie? Yes? Good.' Mum stood up. 'We might go upstairs, then, and get ready for the bushwalk. We have to pack up, too – late checkout is 2 p.m.'

'Oh, but we just sat down,' Dad objected, his hand on Matoaka's arm. 'We haven't had lunch yet.'

'Well, don't let us stop you,' Mum retorted.

'When does the bushwalk start, anyway?' Dad checked his watch. 'It's not for a while, surely?'

'It can take a long time, putting sunscreen on an entire family,' Mum replied, and hustled us off – me, Ray and Bethan. It's the kind of thing she often does when Dad's around. As if she wants us out of the way.

We were climbing the stairs when we ran into Sylvia, who was hurrying down, still clutching her hot chips.

'Have you seen Paul?' she asked. 'He's not in our room.'

'No. Sorry,' Mum replied.

'Oh, dear.'

'Did you check the billiard room?' Mum queried. 'What about the bathroom?'

Sylvia didn't seem to hear. She just kept going. I wondered if Paul was deliberately hiding from her. (It was the sort of thing he *would* do, I decided.) On the way to my own room, I passed Michelle's. To my surprise, the door was open. Michelle was sitting on her bed, fiddling with a handkerchief.

'Hi,' I said, stopping.

She glanced up.

'Oh. Hi.'

'Are you okay?'

She didn't *look* okay. Her face was covered in red blotches. Michelle, however, doesn't much like it when you catch her in an emotional state, because she's normally so elegant-looking. So she just waved her hand, dismissively.

'I'm fine,' she murmured. 'How was the ghost tour?'

'Oh – interesting.' I sat down on the bed beside her. 'No ghosts. I have to tell you, though: remember what we discussed in the Grand Arch, this morning?'

Michelle frowned. 'Uh . . .'

'Remember? That bad smell, up near the sinkhole?'

'Oh. Yeah.'

'Well – Rosemary has a pretty amazing theory about that.'

I went on to describe Rosemary's theory, and how Ray was part Gundungurra, and how he'd felt something grab his leg. Michelle listened intently. After a while, she began to seem more like herself, asking questions and coming up with new ideas. How could we research this 'Mumuga'? What exactly did it look like? Should we send Ray back up to the sinkhole, and see what happened?

'He *is* going back to the sinkhole. In just a few minutes,' I pointed out. 'His adventure caving tour starts from there.'

'Then we ought to go up with him,' said Michelle. 'Do you think a Mumuga would register on Richard's equipment?'

'I don't know . . .'

'Maybe we'll see something on the bushwalk, this afternoon,' Michelle continued thoughtfully. 'We should keep an eye out – especially around the sinkhole.'

I was surprised at the way she had suddenly seized on the whole idea. But I suppose that's not unusual, for Michelle. I've noticed that she'll get all enthusiastic about certain things, especially

116

when her mum starts hanging out with a new boyfriend.

Speaking of Colette, all at once she appeared beside us – there, in Michelle's room – and Michelle's whole attitude changed yet again. Her shoulders slumped, and she gazed out the window.

'Hello, Allie,' said Colette, in a tired voice. She, too, looked as if she'd been crying. Her mascara was smudged, and her hair was dishevelled. 'I asked Sylvester about going home,' she announced, addressing her daughter. 'He says he's already paid for that abseiling tour, but –'

'It's all right.' Michelle spoke quite calmly – almost loftily. 'I don't want to go home now after all.'

'You don't?'

'No.'

'But you said –'

'I want to go on the bushwalk.'

'You do?' Colette's expression brightened. 'Well, that's good. We can do it together.'

'Actually, Allie and I have something we want to investigate,' Michelle replied. It was a mean thing to say, I thought. Colette's face fell, and I wondered if Michelle was deliberately trying to get back at her for spending so much time with Sylvester.

It wouldn't surprise me.

I have to admit, stuff like that makes me very uncomfortable. I suppose you can't help it, sometimes, but I honestly don't understand why people are so quarrelsome. It doesn't improve matters. You start off by scoring points, then you begin playing parents off against each other, and next thing you know, you end up like Paul Klineberg – a real pain in the butt.

'Ah. Allie. There you are.' My mum had stuck her head around the edge of the door. 'Can you come and help pack, please? Your knapsack's here, and all sorts of books and pens and things –'

'I'm coming.'

It was a relief to get out of Michelle's room. After all, I didn't really belong there – not in the middle of a family spat. I escaped by helping Mum and Ray to pack our suitcase, while Bethan bounced around on the beds. Then we all went down to the car park, threw our bags into the car, and finally headed for the reception hall, where Ray settled our bill. I think Joyce or Richard must have arranged to meet in the reception hall, because upon reaching it we hooked up with the rest of the gang: Michelle and Colette, Sylvester (who looked a bit stupid in a pair of stretchy lycra things that were probably bike shorts), Richard, Rosemary, Dad and Matoaka, who wasn't really dressed for bushwalking. She wore a billowy, Indian dress and sandals, while Dad had forgotten to bring a hat. When Joyce arrived, she made him go and get one. 'No hat, no way,' she declared cheerfully.

He came back wearing a floppy rainbow hat, trimmed with a band of cowrie shells.

Joyce herself was dressed in a wide-brimmed Akubra, proper walking shoes, khaki pants, and a Stonehenge T-shirt. She carried a neat little back-pack which she said was full of water, sunscreen, insect repellent and other useful things, including a guide to the Jenolan walking tracks and a book called *Mammal Tracks and Signs*, by someone named Barbara Triggs. At this time of the day, she said, it was unlikely that we'd be seeing any wildlife, except perhaps the odd bearded dragon or skink. But if we kept a sharp lookout, we might spot *traces* of the animals that had passed across our trail recently. Footprints, for example. Or scats.

'Scats?' said Bethan.

'Er . . . droppings,' Joyce explained. 'Dung.'

'Poo, you mean?'

'Yes.' Joyce cleared her throat. 'It's quite possible to distinguish between different types of drop-pings, if you know what to look for.'

I didn't hear what else she said about droppings, because Rosemary came up to me and tapped me on the shoulder. She was wearing a baggy T-shirt over beautifully ironed shorts. There was an eager look on her face.

'I've been thinking about what you told me,' she whispered. 'About my grandmother.'

I have to admit, I'd forgotten about her grandmother.

'Oh, yes?' I said, very quietly.

'My grandmother was always *so* involved in family affairs,' Rosemary told me. 'She loved us all very much, and wanted to know everything we were doing. Maybe that's what's worrying her. Maybe she wants to know what we're doing.'

'I guess.' It seemed like a reasonable explanation to me – especially if Rosemary's grandmother was somehow stuck in Rosemary's room. 'Maybe you should just tell her what's going on, every so often.'

'Yes, but how?'

'I don't know. Go to her grave?' I would have suggested that Rosemary ask Delora for advice, if Delora hadn't once been Richard's girlfriend. 'Why don't you ask Richard?' I suggested tactfully.

Rosemary nodded, just as Michelle came over to find out what we were discussing. But before I could tell her, I was interrupted. Sylvia had approached our group, emerging from the guest lounge. She went straight up to Richard and inquired, in a trembling voice, if he had seen her son.

'No,' said Richard. 'Why?'

'I can't find him.'

'Oh.'

'I've searched everywhere!'

She was still clutching her packet of chips – which can't have been very hot, by that time. Richard rubbed his chin, looking a little confused. Then Mum took matters into her own hands.

'Where *have* you searched?' she inquired of Sylvia.

'Everywhere. The restaurants. The toilets. All those rooms near the bar –'

'The gift shop?'

'Yes.'

'You were about to head off home, weren't you? Have you checked your car?'

Sylvia hesitated. 'N-no,' she admitted.

'Why don't you do that?' said Mum. 'Then, if you still can't find him, you should go to the guides' office.'

'The guides' office?'

'To notify them that Paul's missing.' As Sylvia's face crumpled, Mum stepped forward quickly, and put an arm around her shoulders. 'I tell you what,' Mum said, 'what if I come with you? I'm sure it'll be all right. Paul's probably just hiding.'

'Oh, no!' Sylvia exclaimed, in great distress. 'He wouldn't do that! He *knows* I have to get him back on time!'

I caught Michelle's eye, and we quickly looked away from each other. Personally, I was *convinced* that Paul was playing one of his foul tricks. But Ray cleared his throat, and said gently, 'Maybe he doesn't want to go back. Maybe he wants to stay with you for a bit longer, Sylvia. Have you thought of that?'

Obviously she hadn't. But it seemed to cheer her up a bit. Mum removed the packet of chips from her hand, and gave it to Ray.

'Get rid of these, will you?' said Mum, before turning to Michelle's mother. 'Can you watch the kids for me on the bushwalk, Colette? I do think Sylvia needs some help, here.'

'Yes, of course,' Michelle's mum replied. Then Dad, who was standing beside me, put a hand on my shoulder.

'I can look after them, Judy,' he growled. 'I'm perfectly capable, believe it or not.'

No doubt Mum's snappy answer to this remark was on the tip of her tongue. Luckily, however, Richard stepped in first. He pointed out that it was nearly one o'clock, and that he, Ray, Rosemary and Sylvester were due up at the sinkhole.

Hearing the word 'sinkhole', Michelle immediately informed Joyce that we (namely, Michelle and I) wanted to go to the sinkhole too, before we started on our bushwalk. Would it be possible?

'Why, of course,' said Joyce. 'Anywhere you like. Unless someone else has another preference?'

Nobody did. So the group started to move, with most of us heading out the front door, across the road, to the flight of stairs that marked the beginning of the Six Foot Track.

As we marched away, I glanced back at Mum and Sylvia. Poor Mum. Poor Sylvia. But I doubted that Paul was lost or anything. I was quite sure that he intended to lie low until he'd caused a really major disturbance.

'Maybe Paul got trapped in a cave,' Bethan remarked chirpily. 'Or maybe he ran into the Mumuga, and got eaten.'

'We can only hope,' said Ray.

But he spoke very, very softly, and no one heard him except me.

CHAPTER # eight

By the time we reached the sinkhole, a small crowd had already gathered there. It was a noisy crowd, dressed in brightly coloured clothes; in its midst was the guide – Philip – who was handing around lots of jangling equipment. What with all the commotion, and the bustle, and the large numbers of excited people milling about, I wasn't surprised that we didn't smell anything. No Mumuga, I thought, was going to hang around in these conditions. It was like a railway station platform at rush hour.

'All right,' said Philip, clapping his hands. 'Can I ask if anyone here has ever been abseiling before?'

Ray hadn't. Neither had Richard, Rosemary or Sylvester. So Philip began to instruct them in the proper techniques, until Ray interrupted him with a question about 'possible gas leaks' underground.

'Oh,' said Philip. 'Are you the one who notified the office about a strange smell, this morning?'

'Ah – yes.'

'Well, we've checked it out, and there's no evidence of any problems like that inside the cave. We had a private booking through here at nine, and no one complained.' Philip raised an eyebrow. 'So it's up to you, really.'

Ray decided to go ahead. The others did too. Michelle nudged me in the ribs.

'This is pointless,' she whispered. 'There's too much noise.'

'Too many people,' I whispered back.

'Should we wait until they've gone in?'

'It's up to Joyce.'

'I hope Sylvester's stupid bike shorts split right up the back!'

Colette heard that; I glanced at her, and saw that she closed her eyes briefly. Matoaka also had her eyes closed, but for a different reason. Her palms were lifted in front of her, and her head was thrown back. Possibly she was feeling for totemic vibrations, or something.

'Come *on*,' Bethan whined, tugging at Dad's

hand. My brother always gets bored when he's forced to stand around for too long. 'Let's *go*.'

'Are we ready to start, Joyce?' Dad asked.

'Any time you like, Jim. I thought we'd do a little bit of the McKeown's Valley track, though perhaps not the whole round trip, which is supposed to take about three hours.'

'I don't think the kids –'

'No, of course not.'

'Where's Gordon, by the way? Isn't he coming?'

'Oh, Gordon's knee is playing up, I'm afraid. He couldn't cope with a bushwalk.'

'Bye, Ray!' Bethan shouted, because Ray was disappearing into the sinkhole.

He looked pretty funny in his caving helmet.

'Bye, kids,' he replied.

'It's not fair,' Bethan grumbled, as our bushwalking group began to move away from the sinkhole. 'I *really want* to go with Ray.'

'But you want to go with me too, don't you?' asked Dad.

'No,' said Bethan.

What he meant, of course, was that he preferred caves to bushwalks. Dad, however, probably didn't understand. He said, 'Oh,' very quietly.

For some reason, I almost felt sorry for him.

'There's too much interference,' Matoaka observed, opening her eyes suddenly. 'I can't pick up any trace of ancient energies, right now. Maybe if we all stand still, and concentrate . . .'

'*No*,' Bethan complained. 'Let's *go*.'

Michelle rolled her eyes at me. (She's not much good at little brothers.) Joyce cleared her throat. Matoaka got down on her hands and knees, causing everyone else to hesitate.

'What's the matter, dear?' asked Joyce. 'Are you sick?'

'Oh, no. No, I just need to feel the earth.'

'Why?' asked Bethan.

'In case it's trying to tell me something.'

There was a brief pause. Finally Joyce remarked, 'It won't tell you anything around here, I'm afraid. Too much traffic. If you're looking for animal tracks, you'll have to look off the path.' She opened up her field guide, and showed a picture to Bethan. 'You see?' she said. 'That's an echidna track, and that's a platypus track. Not that we'll see any platypus tracks in this neck of the woods.'

Joyce was very clever. She let Bethan borrow her book, so that he stopped moaning. In fact, when he found all the coloured pictures of animal dung, he began to laugh. I don't blame him, really, because they weren't photographs. Someone had very carefully painted page after page of 'scats': great big brown ones like sausages, little black ones like seeds, long skinny ones like sticks, feathery grey ones, square shiny ones, pale pointed ones, pod-shaped, bean-shaped, nut-shaped . . .

I have to admit, I was just as fascinated as Bethan was. Who on earth had been given the job of painting such pictures?

'Illustrations of scats, skulls and shelters by Anne Breckwoldt,' Michelle read, as she and I jostled Bethan from both sides. 'Poor Anne Breckwoldt. Yuk! What a job!'

'I think it's a *great* job!' Bethan protested. 'Hey – let go! It's not *your* book!'

'It's not yours, either.'

'Kids,' said Dad. 'Let's all share the book, please.'

'I wonder if Ray's ever had to draw animal poo?' I remarked. 'He's had to draw trees, and flowers. They *might* have asked him to draw poo.'

'You see how different all the scats are?' said Joyce. 'It means that you can always tell what might have been in a particular place.'

'Yeah! That's what I want to do!' Bethan exclaimed. 'I want to find some *poo!*'

So we looked. Walking along the sandy track, we kept our eyes peeled for animal pellets. Sometimes Joyce pointed out hollows in the tree-trunks, or clumps of leaves and twigs high in the branches. (These, she said, might be the homes of possums or birds.) Once she stopped to examine what she

128

said was probably a 'rabbit's scrape'. She also told us to watch out for flattened patches of grass in protected areas – these, she explained, were often left by sleeping wallabies, especially if the ground was scattered with droppings. When we found a couple of little holes, Joyce announced that they could very well be echidna 'poke-holes', made while searching for ants.

Our most important discoveries, however, were scats. Dad found two near a tree: they were very small and dry, and Joyce said that they probably belonged to a ring-tailed possum. Then Joyce found another clump, which we all decided must belong to either a rabbit or hare. And Matoaka . . . well, let me tell you what happened to Matoaka.

We were on our way back to Caves House. It was nearly three o'clock, and Joyce had decided that we'd gone far enough. Bethan was still scouring the ground for poo; he had borrowed a plastic bag from Joyce, and was collecting whatever pellets he could (carefully, without touching them with his bare hands) because he wanted to draw pictures of them when he got home. No one else, however, was much interested any more. We were too hot and tired. Joyce was discussing English hotels with Colette. Michelle and I were talking about the Mumuga, wondering whether it really was something that the Exorcists' Club should be following up. A Mumuga wasn't a ghost, after all, though it *was* supposed to be a spirit creature. But if it was a spirit creature, Michelle pointed out, how could it have left such a terrible smell behind it?

'Well – why not?' I asked.

'Ghosts don't smell.'

'Are you sure? I mean, why wouldn't they?'

'Because they don't have bodies. They're made out of air, or – or whatever it is. They're like clouds, or fog. Clouds don't smell either.'

'Yes, but the Mumuga isn't a ghost, is it? Ghosts don't eat people, but spirit creatures do. So they *must* have bodies.'

'Perhaps Aboriginal spirit creatures are like the yeti, or the Loch Ness monster,' Dad suggested. 'They may be real or they may not.'

'Maybe.' I didn't really know what to say to Dad. He seemed to be dividing his time between me and my brother, either helping Bethan to find animal dung or butting into my conversations with Michelle. Sometimes Michelle and I would walk more quickly, hurrying ahead so that we could discuss the Exorcists' Club in private. But Dad always caught up with us. The faster we went, the faster he went.

'By the way,' said Michelle, at one point, 'what *were* you and Rosemary talking about? Back there

130

at Caves House? I could have sworn I heard you mention a grave.'

'Oh.' I explained about Rosemary's problem, and the solution that I had offered. 'What do you think?' I asked. 'Do you reckon it'll work?'

Michelle shrugged. 'It's worth trying,' she answered. 'Only I don't know about going to the grandmother's grave. Not if the ghost is stuck in Rosemary's room.'

'Unless she isn't,' I pointed out.

'Right. But if she isn't, then why didn't she come here last night to bother Rosemary?'

'Maybe Delora would know,' I said.

We both agreed, however, that we probably shouldn't mention Richard's old girlfriend to his new one. Michelle insisted that it would only create a lot of bad feeling, because old and new girlfriends always hate each other. Dad (who had been eavesdropping again) said that this wasn't always true. He said that many people were capable of embracing change in a positive manner; that Matoaka, for instance, liked my mum a lot. The words were no sooner out of his mouth than it occurred to me: where *was* Matoaka?

'Where's Matoaka?' I queried, stopping in my tracks.

Everyone else stopped too. We all looked around. Colette cast her eyes to heaven.

'Not *again*,' she sighed.

We were on a winding, bushy pathway studded with rocky outcrops, not far from the sinkhole. You couldn't see behind you for any great distance; spiky branches were blocking the view. Dad called out: '*Matoaka!*'

There was no reply.

'She'll be all right,' he said. 'She probably wanted to get away from our auras, for a while. They'd be causing interference.'

'There are signposts everywhere,' Colette added. 'She'll be able to find her own way back. It's not exactly the Tasmanian wilderness out here.'

Joyce seemed unconvinced. She peered up at Dad, blinking behind her glasses.

'Yes, but – she wouldn't do anything *silly*, would she?' asked Joyce. 'I mean to say, she wouldn't go climbing on ledges, or sliding down holes?'

It was a sensible question. In my opinion, Matoaka was *exactly* the type who might decide to stand on the edge of a cliff with her eyes shut, swaying back and forth. I turned to Dad. So did Michelle, and Bethan, and Colette. We all waited for an answer.

We didn't get one, though. Before Dad could reply, we heard a scream. It was a distant, muffled scream, but it was a scream.

'Oh, my God,' said Joyce.

The scream was coming from behind us. It was followed by another scream, and then a wail. Dad bolted back down the path, retracing his steps.

The rest of us followed him.

'Is it her?' Michelle gasped, as we slipped and slid over loose stones.

'I don't know . . .'

'Listen.'

This time I recognised Matoaka's voice, because she was actually saying something. 'Oh, *no*,' she was moaning. 'Oh, *yuk* . . .'

She didn't sound as if she was very far away. In fact, upon rounding a corner, we almost ran straight into her. She was hopping along, her face screwed up in misery, the hem of her billowy cotton dress spattered and smeared with something awful.

The nasty stuff was all over her left foot, too; her frail Indian sandal hadn't given her much protection.

'Look what I *stepped* in!' she whimpered. 'Oh, it *stinks*!'

It certainly did. Colette retreated. Joyce whipped out a handkerchief, but she didn't give it to Matoaka; she held it over her nose and mouth.

Dad said, crossly, 'What the hell were you doing?'

'I thought I saw a rock painting,' Matoaka replied. 'Off the path –'

'You're *covered* in that stuff!'

'I fell over!'

'What kind of poo is it, Joyce?' asked Bethan.

'Oh – uh – I don't know, dear. Nothing native. Pig, perhaps.'

'Pig . . . pig . . .' Bethan began to leaf through Joyce's field guide. Matoaka leaned on Dad, holding her dirty foot aloft.

'It was *huge*!' she groaned. 'It was *twice* the size of a cow pat! They shouldn't let cows wander around here!'

'They don't,' said Dad. 'How could they? It's practically perpendicular – *and* it's national park.'

'Did it look like that?' Bethan inquired, thrusting the field guide at Matoaka. It was open at a page showing a series of squashed black boulders stuck together. 'That's pig poo.'

'It was a puddle,' said Matoaka. 'An enormous green puddle of muck.'

'Maybe some bushwalker had diarrhoea,' Michelle remarked, whereupon everyone began to look sick. For a second I felt as if I was going to vomit.

'Oh, *no*,' Matoaka shrilled.

'Shhh!' Dad didn't seem very sympathetic. 'Stop carrying on, it's not going to help.'

'I've got some tissues,' Colette offered. She was quite a long way away, by then. When she gave

Dad her tissues, she had to hold out her hand, and inch across the space that divided them both. After which she quickly retreated again.

'And I've got water,' said Joyce, surrendering her water bottle. With the tissues and the water, Matoaka managed to clean off some of the worst mess. But she still smelled bad – especially when she was in the sun.

Bethan said, 'I don't suppose I can put some of that in my plastic bag –'

'*No!*' we all cried, in unison.

'I wasn't *going* to.' Bethan's tone was impatient. 'I *said* I don't suppose I could – it's much too soft. But if I go and have a look at the puddle now, maybe I could draw a picture of it later.'

'No,' said Colette.

'But –'

'No, Bethan.' Colette spoke firmly. 'You'd stumble about searching until you slipped in it, and your mother would kill me. *No.*'

Dad opened his mouth, then shut it again. I don't know what he might have wanted to say. Bethan complained about Ray taking our camera on the adventure tour, at which point we all began to make our way back to Caves House: Joyce in the lead, with Bethan beside her, asking questions about pig dung ('Why is it that funny shape?'); Michelle and I in the middle, practically treading on Bethan's heels because we were trying to put as much distance as possible between ourselves and Matoaka (who really stank); and Dad bringing up the rear, holding on to his girlfriend, who still preferred to hop along rather than place the sole of her foot firmly on her wet, smelly sandal.

We had only gone a short way when a light bulb seemed to explode inside my head. I had been thinking about the green puddle – I couldn't help it, when the stink kept wafting up my nose – and it suddenly struck me: the poo! The stink! The size of it!

Could it have been *Mumuga poo*?

'Hey!' I came to an abrupt halt. If Dad and Matoaka had been closer, they would have run straight into me. 'Hey!'

'What?' said Michelle.

'The Mumuga! It moves its bowels! Remember what Rosemary said?' I grabbed Michelle's arm in my excitement. 'That stink happens because it keeps *moving its bowels!*'

'You mean –'

'What if it's Mumuga poo, back there?' I was thinking so quickly that my mouth couldn't keep up with my brain. 'If people pass out, if they fall over, then there must be heaps of it! To make the smell!'

'Heaps of poo, you mean?'

'Yes!'

Michelle glanced at Matoaka, who had caught up with us.

'But we're not passing out,' said Michelle. 'And she's got it all over her.'

'Not really. She's just got a bit on her dress, and her foot's been washed. I'm talking *masses* of it. Pool after pool of fresh crap! It would have to be fresh.'

'What *are* you talking about?' said Dad.

'The Mumuga!' I turned to him. 'What if that green puddle was a Mumuga scat?'

'Oh, I – I don't think so . . .'

'Why not? What else could it have been? You said yourself, it couldn't have been a cow pat. And it was too big for a dog, or a fox.'

'Unless it belonged to a pig with diarrhoea?' Michelle proposed, thoughtfully.

'It had to come out of a carnivore,' Bethan declared. He had stopped, turned round, and rejoined us. 'It says in this book that "*a strong odour is also characteristic of a carnivore's scat*".'

'Well, the Mumuga's supposed to eat people,' I said. 'That makes it a carnivore.'

'Maybe we *should* go back and look,' said Michelle. 'Maybe we should even collect a sample, like Bethan wanted to.'

'*No.*' Colette wouldn't hear of it. 'No, no, no.'

'But Mum –'

'I don't want anyone *near* that dreadful stuff!' Colette snapped. 'Good God, are you mad? You heard what Joyce said! You can pick up tapeworms and all kinds of things!'

'Only in dog poo,' Bethan pointed out. 'Dog and dingo. And fox, maybe.'

Colette, however, wouldn't listen.

'It's nearly half past three.' She waved her watch at us. 'The adventure tour should be finished by now, and Judy will be getting worried. We have to go back.'

'But it might be our only chance!' Michelle protested. 'What if it's genuine Mumuga poo? We could have it analysed! It'll be the first Mumuga poo ever found!'

'Oh, don't be silly, Michelle.'

'She's not being silly!' Once again, I turned to Dad. 'Please, Dad! They can go, and we can stay! It won't take long. Please?'

Dad hesitated. Matoaka was the one who answered.

'You can't find that puddle without me,' she grumbled, 'and *I'm* not staying. I need to change. I need a shower.' She tugged at Dad's arm. 'Come on, Jim, this isn't fair.'

Dad looked at her. He looked at me, and at Bethan. He didn't know what to do; you could see it in his face. At last he addressed Michelle's mother.

'Do you think you could help Matoaka get back to Caves House?' he asked doubtfully. 'I can easily find my own way, with the kids . . .'

I grinned at Michelle. We were in with a chance! But seconds later, my hopes were dashed. Colette waved her hands, jangling her bracelets.

'Jim,' she rejoined, 'what is Judy going to say if you turn up late with those kids, and they're covered in slime? Do you really think she's going to be pleased? With me *or* with you?' As Dad frowned, she added, 'You'll be lucky if she lets them anywhere near you ever again.'

Dad blinked. He took a deep breath. Matoaka yanked him forward.

'Come *on*, Jim.'

When he turned to me, I knew I'd lost.

'It's very unlikely to be Mumuga poo, Alethea,' he said apologetically. 'What are the chances? It's more likely to be human.'

'Oh, *please!*' his girlfriend wailed. 'Don't even *say* that!'

'I'd prefer not to upset your mum,' Dad went on, ignoring Matoaka. 'I don't want to . . . to . . . it might make things difficult.' Under his breath, he muttered, 'More difficult than they already are.'

So we lost our chance. We could have collected

a sample of genuine Mumuga scat, and we blew it. Even my brother was disappointed. He wasn't convinced that the Mumuga existed (neither was I, for that matter – not *thoroughly* convinced), but he would have liked to see that puddle, all the same. As for Michelle, she was furious.

'It's just because the stupid woman wants to get back to Sylvester,' she growled, while we trudged along. 'Nothing matters any more except Sylvester. God, my mum is so *pathetic*.'

'What about my mum?' I replied, softly. 'If Dad wasn't so scared of her, he would have stayed. I know he would.'

'They're hopeless,' said Michelle. 'They have no spirit of scientific inquiry.'

'I bet Richard would have stayed, if he'd been here.'

'Do you think so?'

'Richard's scientific. He's interested in things. Maybe we should ask him to help us, when we get back.' The more I thought about this, the more sense it made. Of course! Richard! 'Maybe we could ask him to have a look around, and see what he can find. I bet he would. I bet he'd be really keen.'

But when we returned to Caves House, I was out of luck.

Despite the fact that it was ten to four, the adventure tour still hadn't returned.

CHAPTER # nine

Naturally, Mum was getting worried. The first thing she said to us was, 'Ray's not back yet'. That was after we finally tracked her down in the guides' office. It took us a while.

First we all went to the bistro, because Joyce thought that everyone would probably be there. But she was wrong. No one was there except Gordon. He was sitting by himself with a cup of tea in front of him, reading a newspaper.

He told us that Mum had been rushing around with Sylvia. The last he'd heard, they still hadn't found Paul.

Then he wrinkled his nose and added, 'What's that horrible smell?'

Matoaka made a kind of bleating noise. She tugged at Dad's arm and said, 'Come *on*. I've got to *change*.' I don't think Dad wanted to go with her. He pointed out that she had the car keys, and advised her where to find the nearest tap. That's when she realised that she wouldn't be able to have a shower – because we'd checked out of our rooms, already – and her face crumpled.

'I need soap,' she whimpered. 'I need a plastic bag. I need your help.'

'And I can't leave the kids,' said Dad.

'Oh, you can leave them with me, Jim,' Colette offered. 'Don't worry about that. I'll buy them all a soft drink, or something. I'm *dying* for a coffee.'

Dad didn't look pleased. But then Joyce came to the rescue. 'It's all right, dear,' Joyce said gently, to Matoaka. 'I'll help. You'll need someone who can get into the Ladies with you, surely?'

Even Matoaka could see the sense in that. So she went off with Joyce, as Michelle's mum collapsed into a chair beside Gordon. 'Michelle, my love,' she sighed, 'will you be an *angel* and order Mum a coffee? Skim latte, please. And whatever you want for yourself. And your friends.'

She began to fish around for money in the pocket of her skin-tight jeans. Bethan's eyes lit up. Dad, however, raised his hand.

'I'll get the drinks,' he declared. 'What do you want, kids?'

Bethan wanted an iced chocolate, with lots of cream. Michelle wanted a lemonade. I asked for a vanilla milkshake – to take away.

'Don't you think we'd better find Mum?' I asked Dad. 'She'll be wondering where we are.'

'No need to fret, Alethea. It's only four o'clock.'

'Is it really?' Colette checked her watch. 'So it is. Shouldn't the tour be back by now? I wonder where Sylvester could have got to?'

Michelle flashed me a grimace, as if to say, 'You see?' I didn't know how to respond. Dad went to buy the drinks, and Bethan – who hadn't returned Joyce's field guide – began to show Gordon the pictures of animal scats, until Colette told him to please shut that wretched book, because it wasn't something that he should be reading at the table.

When our drinks arrived, we consumed them quietly. Even Bethan was too tired to talk much. Dad clicked his tongue a couple of times over the food that other people in the bistro were eating. He mentioned the high rancidity factors in canola oil, and how margarine was really a blackish colour until it was chemically altered to turn yellow.

Michelle's mum made a face. 'Please, Jim,' she protested, setting down her empty glass. 'I'm feeling a little fragile, after that dung incident.

143

Are you finished, Michelle? Yes? Then let's find Sylvester. We'll need to go shortly, or we won't get home until late.'

'I'd rather stay with Allie,' Michelle rejoined.

'Yes, I'm sure you would,' said Colette, rising. 'But you can't. As soon as we find Sylvester, we have to leave.'

'Why can't I go in Allie's car?'

'Because you can't.'

'Why not?'

'Because you *can't*, all right?'

I could see by Michelle's stubborn look that there was going to be an argument. Luckily, Gordon stopped it. He shook out his newspaper and said, in a sort of fake-casual voice, 'I'm pretty sure that tour hasn't come back yet. I would have seen them come down the steps across the road. Why don't you all go down to the guides' office, and inquire? If they turn up while you're gone, I can tell them where you are.'

It was a very sensible suggestion. Nevertheless, Michelle's mum insisted on checking the gift shop, and asking at the reception desk, before heading down to the guides' office. Here we found my mum sitting on a long bench, and Sylvia pacing up and down, wringing her hands.

'Ray's not back yet,' Mum announced, the moment she saw us. 'Where have *you* been? It's past four!'

144

'We were on the bushwalk, Mum, where else would we have been?' Bethan shook his plastic bag at her. 'And look what I found! Animal scats!'

'What?' She sounded a bit dazed.

'That's possum, and that's rabbit! I'm going to draw them when I get home. Like in the book.'

'They're poos,' I supplied, when I saw Mum's confused expression. Before she could say anything, however, Sylvia ran up to Colette.

'Have you seen him? Have you seen Paul?' Sylvia quavered.

'Why – no.' Colette was startled.

'You didn't see him on your bushwalk?'

'No, I'm sorry.'

'Oh, my God. Oh, my *God*.' Sylvia put her head in her hands. It was pretty scary – I hate seeing adults get that upset. Mum sighed.

'Come on, Sylvia, calm down,' she said. 'You know what they told us.'

'What did they tell you?' asked Dad.

I was keen to hear the answer as well, but Mum just waved his question aside, impatiently. Sylvia said to Colette: 'They've looked through all the buildings, they've made an announcement over the PA system –'

'He'll be all right, Sylvia,' Mum insisted, not sounding very sympathetic. 'It's only been a couple of hours. I'm more worried about Ray.'

'Oh, really?' Colette frowned. 'Why is that?'

'Because *they're* worried.' Mum pointed at the guides' desk. Behind it, Greg from the ghost tour was talking to another guide, in a low voice. Someone else was on the phone. 'They keep on telling me there's been a bit of a hold-up, but they won't say why. A "delay", they reckon. I can't get anything out of them.'

'What do you mean, you can't get anything out of them?' Colette's voice was suddenly almost as shrill as Sylvia's. 'Sylvester's down there!'

'Yes, Ray too. I pointed that out –'

'Who's in charge? Who have you spoken to?'

'It's hopeless, Colette, they're running around like headless chooks.'

'They're supposed to be looking for Paul!' Sylvia exclaimed. 'He's just a child!'

'Oh, he's trying to scare you,' Colette snapped. 'For heaven's sake, he's a little stirrer. It's all a trick, to make trouble for everyone else.'

Sylvia's jaw dropped. Mum winced. Michelle nudged me as Sylvia struggled for words.

'What a *disgusting* thing to say!' she squawked.

'Sylvia,' Mum said quickly, 'we're all on edge, here –'

'How *dare* you speak to me like that! My son is *missing*, and you stand there – you stand there . . .' Sylvia began to splutter.

146

'Look, I'm sorry, all right?' But Colette didn't sound sorry. 'It's just that we really don't need this kind of prank right now, when we've got a missing tour group to worry about!'

'They're not *missing*, Colette,' my mum corrected. 'They're just –'

'A prank? A *prank*?' Sylvia screeched.

'He's a walking time bomb, Mrs Klineberg!' Michelle's mum put her hands on her hips. 'He's a *troubled kid*, all right? He needs *counselling*. The whole family does, as far as I can see.'

'Oh, *really*?' Now it was Sylvia's turn to put her hands on *her* hips. 'Well you're the expert, I suppose, after that *appalling* outburst this morning!'

'I beg your pardon?'

'Oh, please!' my mum begged. 'Don't – don't –'

'You and Paul's father would get along fine, the way you both inflict your sleazy paramours on your sensitive children!'

Michelle's mum went bright red. I don't know what she said next, because it came out in such a furious shriek. Mum jumped up. Greg moved towards us, hurrying around the edge of the desk. 'Hey!' he cried. 'Hey – hey! That's enough!' The man on the phone covered its mouthpiece with one hand. '*Take 'em outside!*' he roared. Sylvia burst into tears, wailing something about how Paul's father would kill her – he would never let her have Paul ever again.

I didn't see what happened after that. Suddenly Dad was hustling me out the door, into the late-afternoon sunshine. He was pushing Bethan, too. And Michelle. 'Come on,' he said. 'You shouldn't be here.'

He took us across the road, where there were tables and chairs arranged under a concrete shelter shed. I don't know about Michelle, but I was in shock. I mean, my heart was thumping as if it was trying to break out of my chest, and I couldn't breathe properly. Even Bethan looked frightened.

'Did the Mumuga get Ray?' he squeaked, much to my astonishment. (As far as I knew, Bethan didn't believe in the Mumuga.)

'No, no. Of course not.' Dad patted his back, awkwardly, and peered towards the guides' office.

'What about ghosts? What if there are ghosts down there?'

'Don't be silly, Bethan.' Dad spoke sternly. 'Ghosts are just a cultural construct. They can't hurt you.'

I could have told him that they *can* hurt you – that two boys from my Year Six class, Jesse Gerangelos and Tony Karavias, had once been chased into a disused mineshaft by a ghost. But I knew that Dad would only get cross at me if I did.

Instead, I raised a more likely possibility. 'Do you think there's been an accident?' I queried, finding it hard to move my lips. (They felt all stiff and weird.) 'Like a cave-in, or something?'

'I don't see how,' Dad replied, still staring at the guides' office. 'You heard what that bloke said about the caves, yesterday. They're extremely stable.'

'Maybe it's Sylvester's fault,' said Michelle, in a hoarse voice. 'With any luck, he's broken his neck and they're dragging him out. Slowly.'

I have to admit, I was startled. Michelle was serious. She really was. And I'm sure that I didn't imagine the hatred in her tone, because at last Dad looked away from the guides' office. He fixed his gaze on Michelle, frowning.

'Why do you say that?' he wanted to know.

Michelle just sniffed, and fiddled with one of her earrings.

'That's a septic attitude,' said Dad. 'It's going to poison your whole life, if you don't watch out.'

Michelle snorted. '*Sylvester's* poisoning my life,' she rejoined.

'Why? What's he done?' said Dad.

'He's a bastard.'

'Why?'

'Because he *is*. He doesn't want me around, so I don't want him around, okay?'

Michelle folded her arms. Dad scratched his beard. I shrank back, wishing I was somewhere else. There's nothing I hate more than angry voices.

149

'Well,' said Dad, 'all I know is, that kind of mindset is a running sore of bad energy. And it's infectious. Bad energy begets bad energy. What just happened in there – you're a part of it, you know. You're part of the cycle.'

'Oh, *please.*' Michelle rolled her eyes. All at once, she sounded like her mother – or like someone grown up, anyway. 'What would you know about it? You're just like Sylvester, muscling in where you're not wanted. Why should I listen to you?'

Thinking back, I'm not surprised that Michelle spoke her mind like that. It's what she does; she's not like me. I remember once when she said that Bettina had put too much weight on – and Bettina was right there, listening! There's no way I could ever have done the same. Any more than I could have told Dad that he wasn't welcome.

So I was horrified. I couldn't believe my ears. Sitting there, between Michelle and my dad, I thought: What are you trying to do, you idiot, make things worse? For a moment I understood what Dad had been saying about bad energy begetting bad energy, because it seemed to me that we'd escaped the argument inside just to have it flare up outside.

But we were lucky. Before Dad could open his mouth, Bethan exclaimed, 'He's back! Look!' And

150

I turned to see Ray walking briskly down the road towards us.

Boy, was I relieved. Bethan had actually got me worried, talking about the Mumuga. And I also knew that Ray's appearance would probably put a stop to Michelle's conversation with my dad.

Just in case it didn't, though, I jumped up and hurried over to Ray.

'What happened?' I demanded. 'Are you all right?'

'I'm fine,' said Ray, patting me on the back.

'What about the others? Where are they?'

'Oh, they're coming.' He glanced over his shoulder. 'They're up there. See? Near the steps.'

'Was there a cave-in?' asked Bethan, who had followed me.

'No, there wasn't any cave-in,' Ray replied.

'You didn't see the Mumuga?'

'No, I didn't see the Mumuga.'

'What happened?' said Dad – not very happily, I thought. 'There's been quite a panic over you lot.'

'Oh . . .' Ray shoved his hands into his pockets. His skin and clothes were smeared with mud. He looked sweaty and tired, and his hair was sticking up all over the place. I don't think I've ever seen him that messy; normally he's so neat and clean. 'It's not called the Plughole tour for nothing,' he explained. 'The whole experience was like being a bit of food, winding its way through someone's intestines. The only way out is through something called the "S bend". Not at all pleasant. Sylvester had a bit of a turn.'

'A bit of a *turn*?' echoed Michelle. 'What do you mean?'

'Well, he's a big bloke. He got stuck in a tight spot – it *was* pretty hair-raising, you were basically wriggling along – and he had a panic attack. Had to be talked back up to the surface, step by step. Took a while.'

'What's a panic attack?' Bethan queried, with great interest.

'Nothing that's any of your business,' Ray warned. 'I mean it, Bethan – it's not something I want you bringing up, all right? Now where's your mum? It's getting very late.'

Michelle, Bethan and I all started talking at once. At the same time, a small knot of people spilled out of the guides' office. Mum was part of it, along with Colette and Sylvia and Greg. Greg seemed to be pushing the others through the door, ignoring Colette, who was addressing him sharply. Sylvia was wiping her eyes with a tissue.

Mum immediately spotted Ray.

'Ray! You're back!' she cried.

'Yes –'

'They're back! Look!' Mum turned to poor Greg. 'Why didn't you tell us they were back?'

'Perhaps because I was otherwise occupied,' Greg drawled – but I don't think anyone heard him, except me. His reply was drowned by a great surge of babble, as Colette started asking about Sylvester, and Mum started asking about Richard, and Michelle started explaining, with ferocious glee, that Sylvester had 'stuffed up the adventure tour with a panic attack'. Ray, I noticed, shot her a pained look.

'But where is Sylvester?' Colette demanded. 'What happened to him?'

'Nothing.' Ray spoke patiently. 'He's following behind, he had to sit down and do some deep breathing –'

'He got stuck, Mum. He panicked. He ruined everything, the way he usually does.'

'Michelle.' It was Dad. 'Remember what I told you? You're feeding your own misery.'

'Look, Ray! Look at the scats I found! Ray?'

'Yes – hang on a minute, Bethan – Richard and Rosemary went inside Caves House, Judy. I think they were looking for a beer. Is Paul back yet?'

'No! No, he's not! And no one even seems to *care!*'

'Oh, now that's not true, Sylvia, you know the staff's been hunting for hours.' Mum looked around for Greg, but he had disappeared back inside the office. 'Everyone's doing their very best.'

'No, they aren't!' Sylvia cried. 'They think it's all a *prank!*'

This last remark was directed at Colette, who threw up her hands and rolled her eyes.

'I'm sorry I opened my mouth,' she said.

'Yes, but – hang on a minute.' Though Ray spoke quietly, he was obviously concerned. 'Of course, I realise the chances are that he *is* playing a trick. Even so, in these circumstances – I mean, the first few hours are always the most important when someone's missing, aren't they?'

'Oh, my *God!*' moaned Sylvia.

'Ray.' Mum threw a funny sort of look in his direction. 'Could you go and get the kids a drink, or something?'

'We've already had a drink,' I informed her, while Sylvia started to talk about phoning the police. She even pulled a mobile phone out from somewhere or other. Colette was tugging at her daughter's arm. ('We have to find Sylvester,' she was saying.) Mum was trying to calm Sylvia down. Dad kept on butting in, but no one was listening to him. Bethan covered his ears. Ray put an arm around Bethan's shoulder, saying, 'Let's get the kids settled, first . . .'

And then Sylvia's mobile trilled. She got such a fright that she dropped it on the ground.

154

Ray picked it up, but she snatched it from him.

'Hello?' she gasped, pressing it against her ear. *'Hello?'*

As she listened, her expression changed. Her whole body seemed to sag. Michelle turned to me and whispered, 'I bet that's Paul'.

'I – you – you can't . . .' Sylvia stammered. 'That's not true! I would have . . . no . . . how can you . . . I want to . . . wait! Simon!'

Mum caught her breath. She nudged Ray. 'That's him,' she murmured. 'That's the ex-husband.'

'Come on, kids, you come with me,' said Dad, tapping my shoulder. 'We'll go and look at the gift shop.'

I think Bethan would have gone like a shot. But Sylvia suddenly pressed the mobile to her chest and announced, in a broken voice, 'He took him!'

'What?' said Mum.

'Simon took Paul! He came here and took him away!'

'What do you mean, he came here?' asked Mum. 'He came *here*? To the Jenolan Caves?'

Sylvia was so upset that she couldn't explain things very well. Finally, however, we managed to piece together what had happened. Simon, Paul's father, had driven all the way to the Jenolan Caves. When he'd arrived, his son had been on the cave tour, so he'd waited outside Paul's room. Paul had found him there while Sylvia was downstairs buying hot chips. At Simon's suggestion, Paul had left the building with his father, and hopped into Simon's car.

'Without saying goodbye?' Mum gasped. 'But that's terrible!'

'He said I wouldn't have delivered Paul back in time!' Sylvia sobbed. 'He said I was violating the custody arrangements!'

This time it was Ray who tapped my shoulder. 'Come on, kids,' he said softly. 'Time to go, I think.'

We didn't argue.

CHAPTER # ten

In the end, we didn't leave the Caves until after six. There was so much fussing around, you see. Part of the fuss was caused by Sylvia. According to Mum, she wasn't fit to drive – certainly not on the skinny, winding road back to Sydney. So someone had to be found who would stay with her while she calmed down, and called her lawyer, and tried to decide what else to do.

Richard and Rosemary volunteered for that job.

Then there was Sylvester. Sylvester was also causing a bit of a fuss. He was blaming the Jenolan guides for taking people on what he called 'a very dangerous tour'. He said that the Plughole tour had been badly managed, that a man with his enormous muscular shoulders should never have been allowed to take part, that proper warnings should have been issued, that he wanted a refund, that he was going to write to the Department of Tourism, and so on and so on.

Personally, I would have been embarrassed. I mean, why keep reminding people about how scared you were? Especially since it wasn't really anybody's *fault*.

Ray and Richard were sympathetic, at first, but started to get impatient when Sylvester refused to calm down. The word 'claustrophobia' was mentioned, and boy, did Sylvester hit the roof! It was as if he felt insulted. I don't know why. Lots of people don't like confined spaces. It doesn't mean they're cowards, or anything.

Colette finally got mad with him. We were all standing around in the car park, and she threatened to drive off and leave him there if he didn't stop being 'such a baby'. That was after he'd asked Richard and Ray to join him in making a complaint about the Plughole tour, and they had refused to help out.

Michelle was delighted, of course. She drew me aside and whispered, 'Wish me luck. I think Zit-fester just blew it.' That was when she stopped asking if she could hitch a lift home with my family. Don't ask me what her plans were. Maybe she wanted to see what would happen between Colette and Sylvester on the drive back to Sydney. Maybe she was hoping to sabotage Sylvester's attempts to make peace with her mother.

Michelle doesn't seem to mind being in the middle of an argument. She'll even start them, if she feels strongly enough. Personally, I don't know how she does it. I also don't know what she thinks she's going to accomplish.

I think I'd rather live with Sylvester than with endless fights and tantrums.

Then again, I *don't* have to live with Sylvester. Maybe if I did, I'd have a different point of view.

Michelle and her mum were the first to leave. (They took Sylvester with them.) Joyce and Gordon followed closely behind. Richard apologised to the rest of us for the 'unfortunate end' to our weekend away, before wandering off to find Rosemary – who was somewhere in Caves House, holding Sylvia's hand. Poor Richard. You could tell he felt guilty, even though it wasn't his fault. *He* couldn't have known that Sylvester would have a panic attack, or that Sylvia's ex-husband would run off with her son. He also couldn't have known that Matoaka was going to step in a big pile of unidentified manure, and spend the rest of the day endlessly complaining about it – even *after* she'd taken a shower. She and Joyce had snuck into one of the upstairs bathrooms, so that Matoaka could clean herself off using a towel from Joyce's car. But despite the fact that she had washed and changed, Matoaka couldn't stop fussing. She kept talking about 'defilement' and 'purifying her inner space' until Mum told her, quite bluntly, that we'd heard enough about animal dung for one day, thank you very much.

Matoaka took the hint. She didn't have anything else to say, after that.

Unfortunately, Dad did. I thought everything was going to settle down. I was looking forward to a nice, quiet trip home, with only Bethan's restless fidgeting to disturb the peace. But I had forgotten about Dad.

Dad wanted Bethan and me to go home in *his* car.

'It's only fair,' he announced. 'You had them on the way here, Judy, so I should have them on the way back.'

'Excuse me?' said Mum. Ray sighed. Bethan screwed up his nose.

'I don't want to go in your car,' he told Dad. 'There's no airconditioning, and no CD player.'

Dad took a deep breath. 'You won't need them, Bethan,' he pointed out. 'It's cooled off now, and we'll be talking. That's what I want to do. Talk. Communicate.'

'And what about the kids? Suppose they *don't* want to talk?' snapped Mum. At which point Ray said loudly, 'Come on, kids. I think you should both go to the toilet before we leave.'

'But I don't need to go to the toilet!' Bethan whined. (He was still upset about having to give Joyce back her field guide.)

'Yes, you do.' Ray dragged us off to the toilets in Caves House. As we were hurrying away, I could hear Dad growl something about 'materialistic values', whereupon Mum replied, 'Hah! I guess you can *afford* not to have materialistic values, when you spend all your time sponging off people . . .'

'I wish they wouldn't argue all the time,' Bethan grumbled, once we were inside.

'So do I,' said Ray, glumly.

'Mum was never like this before Dad came. Oh!' We were passing the bistro, and Bethan had seen the sweet display on the counter. 'Can I have a chocolate bar? Please? I won't eat it till I'm in the car.'

'Well . . .'

'*Please?*'

'Oh, all right.'

Ray was obviously too tired to argue. So after visiting the toilets with us, he bought two Mars Bars. Meanwhile, I was thinking. I was thinking about what Bethan had said: *Mum was never like this before Dad came.* Basically, Bethan was blaming Dad. We all blamed Dad, all the time. Especially Mum. We were just like Michelle, who was always blaming Sylvester.

I remember standing in front of the bathroom mirror, looking at my reflection. Naturally, I didn't *look* like Michelle. I'm pale with freckles, while she has olive skin. Her hair is smooth, and mine's frizzy. Her eyes are green and mine are blue.

But in some ways, we were the same. She didn't want Sylvester in her life, and I didn't want Dad in mine. Not really. Neither did Mum. Neither did Bethan, when he actually bothered to think about it. It occurred to me that, deep in our hearts, we were probably expecting Dad to just *go away.* He'd gone away once, after all – and stayed away. Why not again? Especially since he wasn't receiving any encouragement. On the contrary. We were all doing our best to make Dad feel unwelcome, only we weren't being quite as obvious as Michelle.

And the result? Well, it was the same result you get when you try to lock Bethan out of your room. I've done that a few times when I've had friends around, and it's like a red rag to a bull. The more you try to exclude Bethan, the clingier he gets. He'll push things under the door, he'll make a great big noise outside in the hallway, he'll play tricks

(*Allie! There's someone on the phone for you!*) and, finally, he'll just stand there whingeing.

I realised that Dad was the same as Bethan. Maybe, I thought, he wouldn't be so pushy if he was getting what he needed. Sort of like a ghost, I suppose. They pester you and pester you and then, when you work out what they want and give it to them, they go away satisfied.

That's what I'd told Rosemary, anyway.

I wondered if going home with Dad, in Matoaka's car, would calm him down a bit. Make him stop arguing with Mum, for instance. And then, if he stopped arguing, Mum might think he wasn't so bad after all, and realise that she could cope with him. That she would *have* to cope with him – somehow.

Mum and Dad were both still bickering when we returned to the car park. It looked that way from a distance, at least. Ray sighed impatiently. He told Bethan and me to wait for a minute, and left us standing on some steps while he went to see what was going on. Bethan said to me, 'Do you think I could open my Mars Bar now?'

'*No*,' I replied. 'Don't even think about it.'

'The paper's a bit torn, look . . .'

'Bethan.' I lowered my voice. 'Do you think you could be nicer to Dad?'

'Huh?'

'You know. Like – going in his car, and stuff.'

Bethan pouted. 'But I don't want to go in Dad's car. He hasn't got a CD player. Or airconditioning.'

'Yes, but it might get him off our backs a bit. I mean, right now he wants to see more of us. Well – if he *does* see more of us, then he'll probably change his mind.' Safe bet for sure, if Bethan's involved. A little bit of Bethan goes a long way. 'It's like with chocolate,' I explained. 'If you eat too much chocolate, you get sick, and you don't want to eat any more for a while. That's probably what will happen with Dad. If we go in his car.'

Bethan frowned. He seemed to ponder. At last, shaking his head, he declared, 'I don't like that car. You can't play CDs. It's only got a radio.'

And that was that. He wouldn't budge. Glancing across at the adults, I saw that they still hadn't come to an agreement. Ray was chewing a thumbnail. Dad was saying something about a 'choice'. Whereupon Mum raised her voice in outrage. 'No,' she said. 'No, Jim, that's not fair. That's too much of a responsibility for them. How can you ask them to make a choice? They'll have to go one way or another and it'll make them feel guilty in either case . . .'

She was talking about my brother and me. God, it was annoying. When I saw Dad fold his arms, I decided that I'd had enough. Someone has to do something, I thought. If not, we'll *never* hit the road.

I walked over to where they were standing and, before they could send me away again, announced that I would go back home with Dad.

For a moment, Mum looked shocked. Then her expression changed. I'm not sure whether I'd hurt her or disappointed her, but I know she wasn't happy. As for Dad, there was no mistaking his smug little smile. In fact, it was his triumphant air that suddenly made me mad.

I guess I was a bit tired, or something. It had been a pretty full day. Anyway, I lost it. I put my hands on my hips and said, 'I'm only doing this to stop you two from arguing. You're worse than me and Bethan – it's like you're stuck going round and round in a circle, doing the same thing over and over again. I mean, you're not ghosts, you don't *have* to get stuck. Neither do I. So maybe if I go with Dad, Dad will stop complaining, and Mum will stop getting mad at him for complaining, and Bethan won't end up like Paul Klineberg, and everybody will just *calm down* because I *really, really* HATE ALL THIS STUPID STUFF!'

I couldn't believe it, afterwards. I couldn't believe what was coming out of my mouth. (Maybe I'd been picking up a few tips from Michelle, without knowing it.) But my own surprise was *nothing*

165

compared to Mum's surprise. And Dad's, too. They just stared at me with their jaws dropped. I guess I never do raise my voice, much. Not like Michelle. I guess I'm usually pretty quiet and sensible.

Then I spoiled it all by starting to cry.

For a brief moment, everything was quiet. I could hear birds calling in the trees around us, and the distant, fading sound of a car engine. Mum and Dad seemed frozen to the spot.

It was Ray who leaned down, gave me a squeeze, and kissed the top of my head.

'You are absolutely one-hundred-per-cent right, my darling,' he announced. 'And everybody here knows it.'

Rubbing my eyes, I saw Mum and Dad both stare at the ground. Dad cleared his throat. Mum surged forward, and gave me a hug.

We left the Caves about five minutes later. Dad went in Ray's car, with me and Bethan. Mum went with Matoaka.

We didn't see any ghosts.

Minutes of the Tenth General Meeting of the Exorcists' Club
Held at Peter Cresciani's House

1.   The President (Alethea Gebhardt) declared the meeting open.

2.   The Secretary (Bettina Berich) read out her minutes from the last meeting.

3.   The Treasurer (Peter Cresciani) asked Alethea for her report on the Jenolan Caves Ghost Tour, which no one had read yet.

4.   Alethea said that she'd written one, but that it was a bit long. She promised to write a short one that everybody could read.

5.   The Publicity Officer (Michelle du Moulin) said that she would write one too.

6.   Bettina asked if they had seen any ghosts, at the Jenolan Caves.

7.   Michelle replied that they hadn't.

8.   Alethea explained that they might have seen *something*, but they weren't sure what it was. Then she pulled out some photographs that her mother's friend Ray had taken underground, while he was on an adventure tour in the Elder Cave. Most of these photographs were kind of dark, and it was hard to make out anything in them – just vague shapes, like the inside of someone's stomach. Two of them showed the mouths of dark tunnels, or holes, that Ray had to squeeze through. In one of the holes, far off in the distance, you could see two round, shiny, yellowish things glinting. Alethea admitted that they could have been two shards of calcite, reflecting the light of the flashbulb.

But they really, really looked like a pair of little yellow eyes.

9.   Mrs Cresciani shouted up the stairs, because afternoon tea was ready.

10.   Alethea quickly distributed copies of a letter she'd received from Richard's girlfriend, Rosemary, in case anyone was interested.

11.   The meeting was adjourned, and everybody ran downstairs to eat Mrs Cresciani's delicious sugared pastries before Peter's brothers managed to finish them off.

Appendix to the Minutes of the Tenth General Meeting of The Exorcists' Club: Letter from Rosemary Prescott to Alethea Gebhardt

Dear Alethea

It was very nice to meet you at the Jenolan Caves last weekend. Richard had talked about you a lot, so I knew how mature and well-informed you were. But I never expected that you would be *such* a big help when it came to my strange dreams about Gran.

It was your opinion that I should probably tell my grandmother what was going on in the family. You said that if I gave her what she wanted, then she might leave me alone. Well, I did exactly as you advised. Three nights ago I sat in my bedroom and quickly ran through the latest family gossip, in a loud voice. On Richard's recommendation, I even held a piece of my grandmother's jewellery while I was talking. And guess what? Since then, my grandmother hasn't bothered me.

I can't thank you enough for your input. I was finding it increasingly hard to sleep, so you've solved that problem. And it's wonderful to know that, at some level, my grandmother still exists – even if it's only in my heart.

Please accept my compliments. Richard has told me about your Exorcists' Club, and it seems to me that you've performed yet another successful exorcism – without going anywhere near the haunted house.

If I can ever help you with anything, please let me know. Meanwhile, I hope to see you at the next PRISM ghost tour.

Yours sincerely

Rosemary A. Prescott

Praise For Allie's Ghost Hunters:

'[*Eloise*] is a very addictive book, and I recommend it to anyone who wants an original mystery story.' Ambrose, Year 8, YARA

'[*Eglantine*] is a delightful spine-tingler and a great read . . .' *Sunday Tasmanian*

'An original twist on an old, old theme . . .' *Sunday Age* on *Eglantine*

'Full of mystery, ghost-busting and humour . . .' *Townsville Bulletin* on *Eloise*

'[*Eloise* is] gripping, creepy and unputdownable.' *Queensland Times*

'Anyone who says they don't believe in ghosts just might be encouraged to think again.' *Reading Time*